ON THE RUN

ON THE RUN

MICHAEL COLEMAN

DUTTON CHILDREN'S BOOKS

NEW YORK

Text copyright © 2003 by Wordjuggling Limited

Library of Congress Cataloging-in-Publication Data

Coleman, Michael.
[Going straight]
On the run / by Michael Coleman.—1st American ed.
p. cm.
First published under title: Going straight. London: Orchard Books, 2003.
Summary: When a persistent youth offender is caught yet again,
he is sentenced to community service as the partner to a blind runner.
ISBN: 0-525-47318-1
[1. Robbers and outlaws—Fiction. 2. Community service (Punishment)—Fiction.
3. Blind—Fiction. 4. Running—Fiction. 5. England—Fiction.] I. Title.
PZ7.C67716O1 2004
[Fic]—dc22 2003063473

Published in the United States 2004 by Dutton Children's Books,
a division of Penguin Young Readers Group
345 Hudson Street, New York, New York 10014
www.penguin.com

Originally published in Great Britain 2003 by Orchard Books,
London, under the title *Going Straight.*

Printed in USA • Designed by Tim Hall
First American Edition
1 3 5 7 9 10 8 6 4 2

For Irene Knowles and Julie Dutty
at the Central Library, Portsmouth, England;
and Pavla Francova, Prague, Czech Republic,
1500-meter and 3000-meter Summer
Paralympic Champion, Barcelona, 1992

ON THE RUN

1

LUKE WAS A THIEF.

His rule of life was plain and straightforward. If he saw something he wanted—he took it. And he wanted most things he saw.

That's not to say that he *needed* them. Luke would have been the first to admit that. He thought of it this way: If he couldn't use what he stole, he could sell it—that was never a problem if you knew where to go—and his family *always* needed money. What he got was his contribution to the family finances. His thieving was a kind of part-time job.

It paid pretty well, too—better than the pittance some of the kids at school accepted for slogging their guts out stacking supermarket shelves or searching the streets for discarded shopping carts. Yes, crime paid, all right.

Of course there were problems, as with any job. "Occupational hazards" he'd heard them called, though his dad had summed it up best:

"It's a game, innit?" he'd once heard him joke. "We nick things and try not to let them nick us."

Luke had been nicked plenty of times. Enough for his name—recorded on the Police National Computer—to be awarded letters after it. Three letters.

Luke Martin Reid, PYO.

Persistent Youth Offender. *Persistent*—meaning so many times that he'd lost count. *Youth*—because he was still under sixteen. And *Offender*—to use another of his dad's jokes—because he'd offended the cops by showing how hopeless they were at preventing him from nicking stuff. Stuff like the bright blue box that had just attracted Luke's attention . . .

JUDGING FROM THE LOGO AND LABELING, INSIDE HE'D find a top-of-the-line and highly desirable (that is, saleable) pair of running shoes. Laid out as invitingly as it was, across the backseat of a smart 4x4 off-roader, the box might just as well have had an additional label on it saying, "Luke, nick me, *please*!"

As if that wasn't enough, the 4x4's undoubtedly well-off owners had parked their wheels in a cozy corner on the ground floor of the multistory parking garage. It was the kind of corner that people bustled past without a second glance. Even better, it was near the shoppers' exit. Just right for a quick getaway. In next to no time, he'd have that box out of the car, the shoes into his backpack, and he'd be melting into the crowd outside.

Luke eased himself alongside the passenger door. Peering down at the ground as if he were looking for something, he snaked out a hand and tried the handle. Locked. Still, he couldn't expect it all to be easy. He'd have to break in.

It wouldn't take long. He was pretty sure this brand of 4x4 didn't have a wailing alarm. Even if it did, it was unlikely to present a problem. With so many of them giving the impression they'd been triggered by a mouse creeping past on tiptoe, people just ignored alarms nowadays.

Hand dipping into his pocket, Luke took a short, apparently aimless stroll toward the exit and back again. By the time he'd returned to the 4x4, he was cradling what looked like a small jigsaw blade between his fingers. A flicker of a smile crossed his face. This was the good bit. The really satisfying bit.

Other thieves might be content with bashing in a car's window, but not him. Too risky. Noisy, for a start. He didn't fancy slicing his hand off, either. Not easy to claim you've never clapped eyes on a car when it's got blobs of your blood all over its plush upholstery. No, busting windows wasn't Luke's way. He got in—*loved* getting in—by picking the door lock. Gently, he slid the jigsaw blade into the 4x4's keyhole. . . .

Luke couldn't remember when he'd first realized he had the talent. It had just seemed to grow with him, like hair and zits. But pick locks he could. Any lock.

If he'd been asked to teach others how to do it, he'd have failed. If his teacher, Mr. Harmer, had said one morning, "Luke, you're a boy worth encouraging. How about giving us all a talk on your extraordinary talent for picking locks?"—well, he'd just have confirmed Harmer's opinion that Luke Reid was a waste of space by failing miserably.

The simple explanation was that Luke *couldn't* explain it. All he knew was that once he slid that blade into any keyhole, it was as if he could see the inside of the lock in his mind's eye; as if pictures were being sent from the tips of his fingers to hidden recesses of his brain, where they were processed and analyzed until the lock's pins yielded to the gentle, but precise pressure that he put on them. Like now.

A satisfying click told Luke that the job was done. Easing the jigsaw blade from the keyhole, he slid it back into his pocket.

That was when they jumped him.

Flushed with pleasure at having cracked the lock so quickly, he'd forgotten the first rule of thieving—check, check, and check again. He'd just opened the passenger door and snatched the box off the rear seat when a powerful arm looped around his neck and yanked his head backward.

"Thanks a lot, kid," growled a voice, with a distinctive throaty laugh. "Saved us the trouble!"

Even as he was being pulled out of the 4x4, Luke was aware of a second person leaping past them. Clambering across to lie on the driver's seat, he began pulling wires out from beneath the dashboard.

"Easy!" crowed the driver. "Come on, Mig! Let's roll!"

That laugh again. "Yeah, yeah!"

In one movement, Luke was released and shoved violently aside. The box flew from his hand, its contents tumbling out onto the oily ground. He had time to feel a pang of satisfaction—he'd been right, the running shoes *were* a top brand, the best he'd ever lifted—before the 4x4's passenger door had been slammed shut and the engine gunned into life.

He'd been mugged by a couple of car thieves! Criminal, that's what it was.

Luke's fists clenched in a reflex action of bitter fury.

They'd caught him by surprise, whoever they were. He peered into the car. He'd remember their faces, just in case he ever got the chance to make them suffer, because that's what he'd do. . . .

The thought died faster than a candle in a hurricane.

In the 4x4's passenger seat, smirking down at him, dressed in camouflage cool, was "Mig" Russell. The big bruiser's nickname came from the fearsome Russian fighter plane. He'd earned it by being just that—a fearsome fighter. And behind the steering wheel—even now reversing the 4x4 out of its parking spot—who else but Lee Young. Ferret-faced Lee Young, who didn't need a nickname because every kid knew what he was. Top gun. Number one.

Lee Young and Mig Russell! At seventeen, they were just a couple of years older than Luke, but in reputation they were veterans. Luke half smiled, half laughed. Jumped by the kings of the East Med Estate! It was almost an honor.

Russell's window oozed down. "What's your name, kid?"

"L-Luke."

From the driver's seat came Young's command. "Yer didn't see us. Don't forget that."

"Or else," added Russell unnecessarily. Young's look had said it all.

The passenger window purred shut. The 4x4 had nearly backed out of its spot now. No squeal of tires, nothing to draw attention to themselves. So cool! Luke felt like asking for their autographs.

"Hey! That's my car! Stop!"

Luke spun around. A man had just come up from the

shoppers' stairway. At his side was a girl about Luke's age. She looked confused, but not the guy—he looked livid. Even if Luke's IQ had been as low as Mr. Harmer was always insinuating, it would still have been high enough for him to work out that here was the owner of the 4x4—and that he wasn't prepared to see it disappear without a fight.

The 4x4's owner was quick on his feet. Leaving the girl standing, he sprinted forward. He got as far as hammering on the rear window before a shocked Lee Young put his foot down and screeched off, tires howling. Without giving Luke a second glance, the guy ran after the 4x4, waving his arms like a maniac.

Luke almost laughed. What did the guy think he could do? Catch up? He didn't even have his flashy running shoes on to help. Then he realized that maybe the guy didn't need to catch up. Earlier, Luke's concern had been about making sure the shoppers' stairway was close enough for him to make his own quick getaway. But cars don't go down stairways. The vehicle exit ramp was in the opposite direction, in the far corner—the 4x4 was heading the wrong way, and the guy obviously knew it.

Even before Lee Young realized the same and began forcing the vehicle into a tire-squealing U-turn around a concrete pillar, the guy had darted to one side and started weaving between other cars. His aim was clear. He was going to try to get in the way and force them to stop.

Luke was transfixed. He knew he should be running himself, out and away, but he couldn't tear his eyes away from the scene unfolding before him. The guy must be mad. He was going to get himself killed. . . .

Then the girl screamed. "Dad!"

She saved the man's life. Her terrified shout seemed to cut through his single-minded pursuit in a way that nothing else could have done. Even as the guy tried to dart through a small gap between a parked van and a concrete pillar—and straight under the wheels of his own 4x4—his head was turning to search for his daughter. It was enough to make him misjudge the gap and clout the pillar with his shoulder.

Luke heard the guy's cry of pain, then saw him double over and drop to his knees. But he was safe. The 4x4 had raced past, well clear of its owner. Seeing this, Luke finally made his own move. The running shoes were still on the ground beside his feet. Snatching them up, he was about to sprint for the exit when another piercing screech of tires caused him to look back.

Luke took in what must have happened in that single glance. An old lady trying to negotiate her way into a parking bay had blocked Lee Young's exit route. He'd been forced to spin the 4x4 into a ninety-degree turn. The suddenness of the turn had caused him to brake sharply. But now he was accelerating again . . . and heading straight for the girl!

She hadn't moved. Confused and terrified, she was still standing where the guy had left her.

"Look out!" screamed Luke.

His shout had no effect. Whether through fear or shock, the girl didn't seem aware of the danger she was in. Even though the 4x4 was roaring closer, the violent sound of its engine echoing round the cavernous parking garage, all she was doing was looking around wildly.

Behind the wheel Luke could see Lee Young. Next to him, Mig Russell had his feet coolly perched on the dashboard. They were glancing at each other, laughing, enjoying the thrill of the steal. Luke could understand that, even if he wasn't in their league. But . . . it seemed to have caused them to lose their concentration. The 4x4 was gunning straight at the girl and they couldn't have noticed.

The girl still hadn't moved. Although her head was whirling from side to side, it seemed as if her legs were rooted to the spot as she continued yelling for her father. But he was in no position to help. Cursing violently, Luke began to race her way.

The 4x4 was surging closer. Surely Lee Young had seen her by now? Hoping against hope that he'd hear the squeal of brakes at any second, Luke urged himself into an extra burst of speed. He wasn't going to make it. . . .

With a wild lunge, Luke half dived and half fell into the girl. At the same time he closed his eyes, bracing himself for the shattering pain of being hit by the 4x4. It didn't come. All he felt was the rush of air as it missed him by a squashed whisker. He heard Young's surprisingly high-pitched laugh. Then Russell yelled a throaty, "See yer, Lukey!" The next moment Luke and the girl were hitting the tarmac together, and she was screaming loud enough to burst his eardrums.

"I'm sorry," gasped Luke. "Honest. I'm really sorry." He scrambled to his feet. Young must have seen them at the last moment and swerved. The girl was safe, anyway, though if she carried on with her yelling she was going the right way about rupturing her lungs. As for her father over on the far side of the parking garage—it looked like he wasn't badly hurt, either. He was merely looking as stunned as you'd expect a guy to look under the circumstances.

Tough, thought Luke. But nobody's been killed. OK, so the girl was still howling and, thanks to the combined efforts of the three of them, the guy was now a 4x4 short instead of just a cool pair of running shoes. . . .

The running shoes. Luke looked around—and cursed. He'd been clutching them under his arm as he ran, like they were jewels he was rescuing from a burning building, but in the collision with the girl they'd gone flying. Now he could see only one of them. He snatched it up, then realized what a waste of time that was. The demand for single running shoes simply wasn't there. Dropping it, he ran.

Within a few strides, he was at the pedestrian exit, almost careering into a woman who'd just come up the short stairway.

The next instant, the woman took in the scene behind him and started screeching herself. "Jodi! Jodi!"

The girl's mother, had to be. As she pushed anxiously past him, Luke glanced over his shoulder—and was glad that he did. The guy was no longer gazing after his stolen 4x4. He was holding the shoe Luke had ditched. Clearly, he wasn't having too much trouble putting two and two together and coming up with the right answer. With somebody else now available to hold his daughter's hand, there'd be nothing to stop him from giving chase. And Luke suspected that a guy who'd just tried to catch a 4x4 wouldn't think twice about coming after him.

Luke raced down the steps, already seeing his route back to the safety of the East Med Estate, the housing project where he lived. It was a good route, too, all dark and little-used back alleys, but this time it looked like he was going to have to take it a sight faster than usual.

Turning left, he hared up the short incline that ran alongside the parking garage. Across the road, a right turn, a short sprint along a rubbish-strewn alley, and he was out onto the worn and pitted road that led to East Med half a mile away. It was a hundred-meter dash before Luke reached his next turning. He stopped and risked a glance behind. The guy *was* following! Luke's early blast of speed had put him well ahead, though. The guy was only just charging across the road.

Luke had reached another alleyway. This one was long and straight, edged by the high and crumbling brick walls at the back of a row of dingy terraced houses. Its disadvantage was that the guy would be able to see him clearly all the way along. On the plus side, the East Med Estate was at the other end. Once he'd reached the sanctuary of its maze of walkways and stairwells, a sniffer dog on Rollerblades wouldn't be able to track him down.

Luke began running again, but not as quickly as before. His legs had started to ache a bit. Within another hundred meters, he'd slowed even more and was gasping for breath. Another glance behind. The guy was closing in on him!

Gritting his teeth, Luke tried to force his legs into action.

They didn't want to go. It was like trying to run in a swimming pool. The more effort he put in, the slower he seemed to move.

He began to panic. The guy was getting nearer by the stride. Any second now, he'd be up to Luke's shoulder. Cursing himself for being so stupid as to try and nick the shoes of an Olympic runner, Luke did the only thing he could think of—he stopped running and started climbing.

Launching himself sideways and upward, he looped his hands over the top of the crumbling, moss-covered alley wall. Slipping and scrabbling for a toehold, he levered himself up toward the top. If he could only get over, he'd have a chance. . . .

He'd just gotten a firm grip on the top of the wall when the guy caught up and grabbed him by the ankle. Luke tried kicking out. It was no use. The guy was showing all the signs of being a wrestling champion as well as an Olympic runner. Digging his fingers in hard, Luke lashed out with all his might in an effort to shake the guy off.

It was too much—not for the shouting 4x4 owner, but for the ancient wall. With a dull cracking sound, the brickwork gave way. Luke fell backward, landing heavily on the guy's leg just an instant before large lumps of moldy brickwork toppled down onto both of them.

Luke gave up. The sharp snap of a bone, the guy's screams of pain, the angry house owner leaping through the gaping hole in his wall, the nosy neighbors running out to see what was going on . . . Luke couldn't escape from them all.

It was almost a relief.

2

THAMES REACHES BOROUGH PRIDED ITSELF ON THE SPEED and efficiency of its youth justice system. Get arrested anywhere else in the country and it could be months before you appeared in court. Thames Reaches' proud boast was that their young troublemakers were up in front of a magistrate within weeks.

In Luke's case, the system excelled itself. Within two weeks, letters were winging their way to various destinations. One of them, addressed to *Mr. A. R. and Mrs. T. M. Webb,* plopped on to a threadbare front doormat on a Thursday morning.

"Theresa! Mail!" Allan Webb called out.

Normally, he would have gone to the front door himself. But then he wasn't normally to be found stretched out on a sofa, his right leg encased in plaster from heel to thigh. He winced as he moved it into a more comfortable position—knowing that inside ten minutes it wouldn't feel comfortable any longer. And, for the umpteenth time, Allan Webb cursed the kid who'd been responsible.

Out in the hallway, Theresa Webb bent to pick up the official-looking envelope at virtually the same moment as the pounding, bass-boosted music coming from her daughter's room was turned up another notch.

"Jodi," she called out, "turn that down a bit, please!"

No answer.

"Jodi!"

Still no answer. Experience telling her that she had no alternative, Mrs. Webb climbed the stairs and rattled on the nearest door. "Jodi! Will you please turn that down!"

The door swung open. "What?"

"I said, will you please turn that down!"

"Sorry. Didn't hear you."

Jodi Webb laughed, knowing the calming effect it always had on her mother. She dabbed a finger on the remote control in her hand and the volume sank below the pain threshold.

"I don't know why you have to have it on so loud."

"It helps me concentrate. I was finishing off the history work you gave me." Jodi smiled again. "That's the answer, Mum. If you don't want loud music, don't give me any work. Better still, don't educate me at home."

She'd tried to make the last part sound like a joke, but Jodi knew she'd failed. It was as if the air between them had become chilly.

"If you bring that work down, I'll mark it for you now," said Mrs. Webb. She didn't move as Jodi turned back into her room. "You want me to wait?"

"No, thank you, Mum! I know the way!"

Plucking up the typewritten pages—accurate, Jodi hoped, if her loud-music-equals-concentration argument was to carry any weight—she closed the door of her room. With the slightest of touches on the knob at the end of the balustrade, she swung round the end of the landing, skipped down the stairs and into the small living room.

Theresa Webb was sitting beside her husband. Allan Webb was reading the letter, the ripped envelope tossed hurriedly aside.

"That—thief. Luke Reid. He's up in court next week. Friday."

"So soon?" Mrs. Webb looked anxious. "Are you going to be able to walk by then?"

"There's no way I'm going to let that lowlife get off. Theresa, every week there are bits in the paper about cases being abandoned because witnesses don't turn up. I'll be in that court if I have to crawl there."

Jodi had put her history work down and seated herself at a small square dining table just inside the door. A pack of playing cards was still there from the previous evening. Giving the cards a quick shuffle, she carefully began to deal them for a game of solitaire. "What will happen to him?" she asked.

"Youth detention or whatever they call it," snapped her father.

"Locked up, you mean?"

"That's exactly what I *do* mean. The cop who took my statement said that he's got a record as long as your arm. Had chance after chance."

Slowly, thoughtfully, Jodi moved a red six up to a black seven. "But . . . he . . . what he did. Pushing me away from the car. Won't that count?"

Mrs. Webb stood up and moved to Jodi's side. "It might. But we hope it won't."

"Why not?" Jodi asked her abruptly.

"Because he probably only did it to save his own skin," interjected Mr. Webb angrily. "Realized if you'd been hit he'd have been in even bigger trouble than he was. Didn't hang around afterward, did he?"

"Sometimes I wish you hadn't chased him, Allan," sighed Mrs. Webb.

"And let him get away with it? No chance. That's what they want. That's why he was so scared when I went after him. Went like a rabbit, till he ran out of steam."

Mrs. Webb leaned across the table in front of Jodi. "Black five here. I'll move it over to the red six for you."

Jodi felt a flash of irritation. "Mum, please!"

"Only trying to help." Mrs. Webb moved reluctantly back to the sofa. "What else did it say?" she asked her husband. On the floor beside him were other pages that had been inside the envelope.

"Nothing relevant. Stuff about what else they could get Reid to do. Meet us, trot out weasel words about being sorry, do some community service. Soft-soap stuff!"

I'm sorry. Honest. I'm really sorry.

Luke Reid's words to her in the parking garage. Despite the terror of the moment, Jodi had heard them. More than that, the words had been flitting in and out of her mind ever since. She turned toward her parents.

"Would it make a difference if he said he was sorry?"

"No. Because that cop said he's going down. He's had all the chances he's going to get."

"Maybe another chance is all he needs, Dad."

Mr. Webb rapped his plaster cast angrily. "Another chance? Jodi, it'll be months before I can run again! Hasn't that sunk in yet? That thief didn't just wreck my leg. He's done the same to our dreams!"

Our dreams, Dad? thought Jodi. Or yours? Do you really know what my dream is?

She turned back to her game of solitaire. Normally she enjoyed the challenge, but not this time. Her mind wasn't on it. An idea was taking shape.

Could it work? Maybe they were right. Maybe this Luke Reid really was a lost cause.

I'm sorry. Honest. I'm really sorry.

And maybe he wasn't.

Persuading her parents wouldn't be easy, though. She'd have to grit her teeth and tug on the tight emotional ties she'd spent so long trying to loosen.

Phrases flitted through her head. *I know it's asking a lot. Please. Do it for me.*

Jodi gritted her teeth. "Mum. Dad. Can I say something?"

3

LUKE TROD THE FAMILIAR PATH THROUGH TOWN TO THE squat white building housing the magistrate's court. Once inside, he presented himself to the public defender.

The public defender, the helpful handout he'd been given by the police had said, as if he didn't know it all by now, *is a lawyer at the court whom you can speak to for free.* So what else was he going to do? Pay big money for a big-shot lawyer? He'd have to rob a bank to do that, which would mean he'd then have to hire an even bigger-shot lawyer to get him off, which would mean he'd have to rob an even bigger bank . . .

Luke drifted over to the small room provided for the public defender's use. The door had a slot for a white plastic plate bearing the name of the day's lawyer—NATHAN DORKING, LLB (HONS).

He knocked and strolled in. Public defender Dorking looked up. In Luke's experience, public defenders were either gray-haired and ready to retire or young and passing through. Nathan Dorking was of the second type. Fresh-faced, but not exactly oozing sympathy. Luke felt like he could read his mind. *I'm here, doing well, going places—not a dead-end drifter like you, thank God.* Dorking waved a hand at a chair and asked Luke's name.

"Luke Reid."

Dorking threw a resigned look beyond Luke, to verify that nobody was about to follow him through the office door. "On your own?"

Luke nodded. "Mum couldn't find anybody to look after my brother and sister." Again.

Dorking accepted the news without much surprise. A fifteen-year-old turning up to face trial without the support of either parent was all too common.

He thumbed quickly through a file he'd drawn from a pile at his elbow, muttering aloud as he read what was obviously a copy of Luke's previous convictions record. "Shoplifting, car crime, vandalism . . ." Then Dorking stopped to check another sheet, presumably one to do with today's case. The public defender sniffed and slapped the folder shut. "I take it you're pleading guilty?"

"Done all the right stuff, have they?" asked Luke.

"If you mean," said Dorking sourly, "can I get your case adjourned because somebody hasn't filled in a form properly, then the answer's no. I don't play that sort of game."

Pity, thought Luke. He'd heard of smart lawyers who'd come up with every reason under the sun for having a case put off, doing it so often that witnesses stopped turning up and the case was scrapped. They probably needed paying to do that, though. It didn't come for free.

"Don't have much choice then, do I?" Luke shrugged without bitterness. "They both saw me there, the guy and the girl."

"The girl?" Dorking frowned.

He seemed about to say more but, after reopening the file for another glance at a paragraph that had been boldly underlined, clearly thought better of it. Instead, he repeated his first question in a slightly different way, as if Luke were a newcomer who needed things spelled out for him, rather than a youth-court regular who'd almost qualified for a season ticket.

"So let me be clear about this, Luke. You do not propose to waste the court's time by pleading not guilty?"

Luke sighed. He was starting to get the impression he'd been in court more times than the public defender. "No," he said. "Not since they're only doing me for *getting into* that 4x4 I won't, no."

"And for the attempted theft of a pair of running shoes," added Dorking.

"Yeah, and that." Luke leaned forward, trying to look more wised-up about the law than he felt. "But if they *do* try to say I was in on stealing that car, it'll be a different game. I'll deny *that*. I had nothing to do with it. I told 'em that at the station."

It had been the nastiest part of the grilling the police had given him. Nastier even than trying to scare him by telling him that the crumbling wall had broken the guy's leg and that they were thinking of doing him for "grievous bodily harm." But in the end they'd had to admit that they didn't have enough to go on. As Luke had argued, neatly he thought, he'd taken the shoe box *out* of that 4x4, hadn't he? If he'd been helping to steal the car, he'd have climbed in *with* them, wouldn't he?

The public defender tilted back in his chair, hands behind his head. "The police accept that you weren't a party to stealing the vehicle, Luke. But they do want to catch the pair who did and—more importantly—almost ran down two people."

It wasn't like that, Luke wanted to say. Lee Young braked and swerved. He must have. But that would have opened himself up to even more questioning about who'd been at the wheel. Besides which, there was a chance that the incident could help him. "I pushed that girl out of the way," he said. "Don't that count for something?"

"It might. I'll make as much out of it with the magistrates as I can. But it won't count as much in your favor as something else would."

"What's that?" asked Luke, pretending not to know the answer.

"They think that you might be able to name names for them, Luke." Dorking had let the chair flop forward again and was staring straight at him.

Luke shook his head, unfazed. "I never saw them, Mr. Dorking. Not properly. That's what I told them at the station. It's all on the interview tape."

The interview. He'd done all right, if he did say so himself. His mum had just sat in a corner—no help at all, as usual—having sighed and said, "Yes, I waive his right to have a lawyer present. Just get a move on. I've left my other two kids with the woman in the flat next door. . . ."

So he'd had to cope on his own, answering their questions without giving anything away.

———

"*TELL ME WHAT HAPPENED, LUKE, IN YOUR OWN WORDS.*"

"*Nothing much. I got in the car, lifted the shoe box, started to get out again.*"

"*Then?*"

"*I was grabbed from behind. Two of them, there were. They shoved me out of the way, got in the 4x4, and drove it off.*"

"*Can you describe them?*"

"*Didn't get a good look at them.*"

"*The car owner says he saw you talking to them.*"

"*They shouted at me. But that don't mean I got a good look at them.*"

"*Come on, Luke. You must remember something.*"

"*Well . . . they were men. Two men.*"

Doubtful tone of voice from the officer. "*Men? Not teenagers?*"

"*No.*"

"*How old were they then? Roughly?*"

"*Pretty old. About twenty-five.*"

"*What were they wearing?*"

"*Er . . . clothes?*"

Irritated tone of voice from the interviewing officer. "*I didn't think they'd be in the nude, son. What sort of clothes?*"

"*Dunno, really. Dark clothes. I'm telling you, I didn't see 'em. . . .*"

IT HAD GONE ON LIKE THAT FOR A WHILE. THE INTER-viewing officers had been tearing their hair out by the end, but still he'd given nothing away. He'd played by the rules of

East Med. No grassing—no ratting on anyone. He'd seen the graffiti on the high-rise walls, same as everybody else: *Death to all grass scum*. If he'd been stupid enough to blurt out the names of Lee Young and Mig Russell, he'd have deserved everything he got. They'd have seen to that. You didn't get to their position by letting kids take liberties.

No, Luke had held out. He'd done the same at a later session as well, when they'd sat him in front of a computer screen and showed him faces of men in their twenties. Crafty sods, they'd slipped Lee Young's mug shot in the middle of them. Luke had been expecting it, though. He hadn't cracked his face, just shrugged and punched the key to bring up the next villain.

DORKING GAVE A RESIGNED SIGH. "SO YOU'VE GOT NOTH-ing to add to your statement, Luke? You haven't remembered any more since then?"

"No, I haven't! What do you want me to do, make something up?"

"Of course not," said Dorking.

"I told them. Two men. That's all I can say."

"Not according to Mr. Webb."

The Olympic runner. "So, what does he say?"

"He's fairly certain that they were teenagers. Seventeen, eighteen perhaps. Unfortunately, he didn't get a good enough look at them to warrant bringing in a few likely candidates for an identity parade."

Too busy running into a concrete pillar, thought Luke. Pity he didn't run into it headfirst.

"Could they have been teenagers, Luke?" Dorking was trying his stare again. This time it worked. Luke found himself shoving his hands in his pockets, lounging back in his chair, staring down at his feet—anything to avoid the public defender's penetrating gaze. He would not, *could not* reveal the names everyone was after.

"Looked like men to me," he said finally. "And that's my last word."

Dorking sighed. "Pity. A couple of names might have helped sway the magistrates. It might have given them a reason for not imposing a custodial sentence."

Luke couldn't help it. He gasped as Dorking said the words—words from the helpful handout that he'd never before taken seriously. *Custodial sentence—a punishment in which you are locked up in a young offenders' institution for at least four months.*

"Lock me up? For a pair of shoes? They can't do that!"

Dorking picked up Luke's file and flapped it like a broken wing. "Not just for a pair of shoes, Luke. For this lot as well. Vandalism, shoplifting, car crime, petty pilfering—not once, but time after time. You're a Persistent, aren't you?"

Luke said nothing. He didn't want to hear all this, even for free. He wanted some encouragement. He wanted to hear that he'd be looking at a few cushy hours sweeping leaves from gutters. He'd happily settle for a scabby sentence, like scrubbing walls clean of graffiti. Especially graffiti like *death to all grass scum.*

But public defender Dorking wasn't in an encouraging mood. During his training, he'd been told that he'd come up against cases like this and should keep an even and civil tone at all times. Fine. But nobody had ever told him that he couldn't give it to the client straight.

"Luke, you've been given cautions, final warnings, community service orders . . . all the *soft* punishments," he added heavily. "I may be wrong, but in my opinion you've left the magistrates no choice. Custody it'll be. Unless . . . " Dorking's voice trailed away, leaving the words unspoken. Unless you name names. Become a grass—an informer. The lowest of the low.

Luke stayed silent. What could he say? That the Webb guy was right? That his 4x4 had been taken by the teenage kings of East Med, a pair who'd reached that exalted position by dealing severely with people who didn't play by the rules?

"I'll do what I can for you, Luke. But I don't hold out much hope." Dorking stood up. The interview was at an end. He stepped across to open the door. "You need to report to the court usher now—but then, I'm sure you know that. I'll see you later."

"ALL RISE."

Luke stood up. For once, he wasn't mildly irritated at the court usher's brusque command, didn't think it was like his school with their old-fashioned ideas about kids "showing respect" by leaping to their feet the instant a teacher came into the room. He was still reeling about what public defender Dorking had said earlier.

A custodial sentence. Locked up. And he knew where it would be. Markham Young Offenders' Institution. He'd heard about other kids on East Med being sent there, like it was a special school set up for their benefit. Everybody knew Lee Young had been in there, bragged about how tough it was—and how much tougher the place had been by the time he'd left.

The three magistrates came into the court. In the past, Luke hadn't paid much attention to who they'd been. One old fogey was the same as another. He didn't care that they were doing the job voluntarily, seeing it as their way of helping young people in trouble. So long as they did no more than give him a lecture and a fairly painless punishment, it didn't matter who they were or what their reasons were for being there. But today was different. If Dorking was right, these three were going to have him shut away in Markham.

"Be seated."

Next to Luke, public defender Dorking ceased standing to attention like a guardsman and eased himself back onto his padded chair. Opposite them, the three were taking their places behind a long teak table. It was on the same level as theirs, not on a raised platform like it had been a while back, somebody having decided that the sight of magistrates looking down from on high was too scary for young muggers and vandals. Apart from the solemn-looking blue velvet curtain behind the magistrates' table, they could have been sitting in an unusually neat head teacher's study.

Luke sat down, too. He knew it was hardly worth the bother. The moment the magistrates were settled, the court usher was hauling him to his feet again.

"Will the defendant please rise."

Mr. Dorking gave Luke an unnecessary nudge. Luke knew he was the defendant. He knew the whole procedure—or so he thought. The clerk of the court, a small man with a squeaky voice, read out the charges. How did he plead, guilty or not guilty?

"Guilty, sir."

Luke had been told that the "sir" part helped get the magistrates on his side. Just like the collar and tie, decent trousers, and polished shoes he was wearing, even though they made him feel like he was encased in plastic wrap. He'd never believed any of it made a scrap of difference, but today he was hoping like mad that it really did. *Luke Martin Reid, we have decided that we couldn't possibly send a lad with such shiny shoes to be locked up in Markham. . . .*

"Thank you, Luke. You can sit down again. Mr. Dorking, what do you have to say?"

The speaker had been the magistrate in the center of the three—a woman with thin lips and hair like fluffy chocolate mousse. On her right was a youngish man wearing a smart blue suit. The third magistrate was much older, with a wrinkled face and the air of a man who'd always looked for the best in people.

Dorking stood up and launched into a short speech about how he'd discussed matters with the defendant and was confident that Luke realized the error of his ways. It sounded to Luke like a public defender's duty speech, one that, judging from the bored looks on the magistrates' faces, they'd heard plenty of times before. But when Dorking mentioned how Luke had helped Jodi Webb, they nodded encouragingly, doing so again when he added, "I would also ask the bench to give the defendant some credit for having pleaded guilty."

"Thank you, Mr. Dorking," said Mrs. Mousse in a kindly tone that gave Luke some hope.

The public defender sat down. Luke glanced his way. Dorking was already leafing through the papers for his next case.

At the table opposite, the magistrates had gone into their usual huddle. This was standard procedure, Luke knew. What he'd heard was that they decided which punishment to dish out before they even got into court. The huddle was just to make sure nobody had changed his or her mind after hearing what they'd heard since. Usually, it was a case of sharp nods and straight into the sentence they'd cooked up for him.

But this time it was different. All three magistrates looked unsure about what to do. Mrs. Mousse in the center was fingering a sheet of paper that the other two magistrates were also looking at. Finally, receiving signs from them that were halfway between shrugs and nods, she turned her attention to Luke.

"Luke, let me ask you something. If you were sitting here instead of me . . . what punishment would you give yourself? What do you think you deserve?"

The question stunned Luke. For just about the first time in his life he didn't have a ready answer. He knew what he wanted—anything except a four-month spell shut up with the hard nuts and psychos in Markham—but as to what he *deserved* . . .

All he could do was murmur, "I dunno, ma'am."

Mrs. Mousse changed tack, or so Luke thought. "Do you see this symbol? Look at it carefully."

She'd turned and was pointing at the blue velvet curtain behind them, leaning to one side so that he could get a clear view of the important-looking coat of arms stitched on it— a lion and a unicorn, facing each other on either side of a big shield.

"Do you see the words at the bottom? Do you know what they mean?"

Luke looked at the scroll winding along the bottom of the coat of arms. *Honi soit qui mal y pense.* He shook his head, trying not to look as if he didn't care that he didn't know.

"Very roughly," said Mrs. Mousse, "those words mean 'Shame on him who has evil thoughts.' It's a reminder that we're here to make sure you're ashamed of what you've done." She turned fully back to Luke and asked, "So—are you?"

Luke knew the answer to that one. "Yes, ma'am. I am," he said, with all the feeling of a persistent offender who didn't want to be locked up. He fooled nobody.

"I doubt it." Mrs. Mousse's thin lips tightened until they almost vanished. "Judging from your appalling record, I doubt it very much."

Exchanging glances with her fellow magistrates, she continued, "All three of us feel the same way—which is why, had it not been for this letter, we would now be sending you to a young offenders' institution. . . ."

Luke's eyes locked on to the sheet of paper between the magistrate's fingers, the sheet they'd all been looking at. A letter? Who from? Who cared—if it was going to keep him out of Markham!

"Listen carefully, Luke," said Mrs. Mousse. "It's in your own interest."

Luke sat up straight, hoping he looked attentive—which he was. He still hadn't a clue as to what this was all about. In a slow, pleasant voice, as if she were at the bedside of a restless child, Mrs. Mousse began reading:

> "To *whom it may concern, Youth Magistrate's Court*
> *Re: LUKE REID*
> *We have been told by the police that Luke Reid has been charged with breaking into our car, but that he wasn't involved in its theft.*
>
> *We have also been told that he's been in trouble many times before and that this time he's likely to be sent to a young offenders' institution.*
>
> *However, bearing in mind that Luke Reid did at least come to Jodi's aid before running away, we would like to suggest a different punishment. We understand that the court could sentence him to work on a project, showing him the effect his criminal activities have on others. . . ."*

Luke's spirits began to soar. What were they going to suggest? It had to be better than Markham, whatever it was! Keeping his attentive look on Mrs. Mousse, he tried not to smile. Moments later, he couldn't have smiled if he'd wanted to.

"Our proposal is that Luke Reid should spend some time working with one particular group of people. This is a group that our family has been involved with for some time—the visually impaired."

Luke had to think for a moment what "visually impaired" meant. Then it came to him. Blind. He was being asked to work with blind people. Why?

Mrs. Mousse laid the letter down. "It is signed by the Webb family," she said directly to Luke. "Mr. and Mrs. Webb and their daughter, Jodi. In my view, a quite remarkable family."

She glanced once again at the other two magistrates. Both nodded. Halfheartedly, but they did it. "So, Luke, that is what we propose to do. We are going to give you what's called a detention and training order. Normally this would mean that you'd spend the first two months locked up; you'd be released to work in the community for the second two months. Well, we are going to reverse that. As the Webb family has suggested, we're asking you to work alongside them for the first two months. If, at the end of that time, your supervisor gives you a good report, then you'll continue that work for the second two months as well. A bad report means that you'll be locked up. It's a very unusual step we're taking, and one that I don't mind telling you we're very unsure about."

Mrs. Mousse paused, letting her words sink in. Finally she said, "We can't make offenders meet their victims, Luke. You have to agree to it. So . . . *do* you agree?"

Agree? Luke didn't know what to say. His mind was still reeling. Meet the runner guy and his drippy daughter? That would be no joke. When he was out thieving, the people who actually owned the stuff he stole never came into his mind. And, on top of that, they wanted him to work with *blind* people?

Into the jumble of thoughts came a sharp whisper. Mr. Public Defender Dorking had leaned across and was almost biting his ear off. "It's that or you're on the next bus to Markham. Up to you."

Put like that, what else could he say? "Yes, ma'am. I agree."

Mrs. Mousse showed no reaction. The stiff head of hair simply dipped a bit as she said, "Very well. And Luke—I suggest you take this chance to keep your freedom. It's the last you'll get."

"Thank you, ma'am." Luke knew the script.

"Before I dismiss you, do you have anything to say? Is there anything you're unsure about?"

Luke hadn't intended to say anything—he never had before. Say nothing and they can't use it against you, everybody knew that. But a thought was still bugging him, and he couldn't contain it. So he asked, "Why blind people?"

Mrs. Mousse picked up the Webb family's letter again. Soon she and her fellow magistrates would be seeing the next offender on what often seemed like an endless conveyor belt of young criminals. All too often they saw the same faces again and again, as if either they couldn't or wouldn't jump off the conveyor. But once in a while she felt a glimmer of hope. Now was such a moment.

"This should answer your question, Luke," she said. "It's the postscript that the Webb family added to their letter:

"Jodi asks that until Luke Reid accepts our proposal, he shouldn't be told that she has been totally blind since she was an infant."

4

LUKE REPORTED TO THE PLACES HE HAD TO REPORT TO
and filled in the forms he had to fill in. By then it was almost
midday. Perhaps he'd go into school for afternoon registra-
tion; perhaps he wouldn't.

He wandered out of the courthouse and headed for the
Bridge. That's what everybody on their side called it, maybe
because it made the footbridge that separated the Old Town
from East Med Estate sound more glamorous than the rusting, peeling reality. But then even "East Med," in conjuring up
images of the sun-soaked Mediterranean, did the same thing.
It was short for East Meadows Estate, most likely because
daisy-filled meadows were what had been plowed up to make
way for the estate's concrete high-rises and boxlike houses.

Walking across the Bridge was like leaving a fertile land
for a desert. Although the big stores had all moved out now,
the Town was still the place to be. It had all the entertain-
ment, all the social life—and much of the money. A "Town"
address, even if it was way out on the northern fringes, said
you were a different class. Respectable.

Stepping onto the Bridge, Luke left all that behind. Sometimes he'd stop at the very center, looking down on the six-
lane expressway far beneath his feet, wondering how
the place must have looked in years gone by. Then he'd walk

on. By the time he reached the other side, he was officially treading on East Med ground. It even felt different.

East Meadows Estate had originally been built for workers in the factories and docks alongside the River Thames, no more than three miles to the south for any crow that fancied the flight. For a while, it had been a vibrant area, attracting workers from far and wide—but only for a while.

Then the industries had faded and collapsed, their workers left without work. As people left the area, East Med had become more and more run-down. Soon, only those who wouldn't, or couldn't, escape were left. Luke had been born around that time.

Finally, when he was six or seven, something had been done. With all hope gone that they'd ever again hum with life, the deserted factories and the docks were flattened. In their place arose Riverside: a vast new shoppers' paradise, brimming with must-haves. The fact that for the majority of East Med's residents the goods were can't-afford-to-haves appeared not to matter. Riverside paid its way by attracting shoppers not only from the Town—of course—but from far and wide. Every weekend they'd come, by car and bus, attracted to the mall like wasps to a jam jar.

The Bridge now behind him, Luke ambled on through the good part of East Med. Here there were new houses, not palaces but better by far than the rest of the estate. The small front gardens had grass rather than layers of windblown rubbish, and, poking out of the earth, there were shoots of daffodils and crocuses instead of bricks and corroded bicycle parts.

Luke felt his usual shaft of anger. When would it be their turn to live in a place like this? His mum was always saying the day would come, the whole estate was being pulled down and rebuilt. It was true. Having put Riverside first, somebody somewhere had found a conscience and decided that it was time to build some decent housing. So now, like one of those paintings by numbers, the ugly gray areas were slowly being colored in by red houses and green gardens.

Maybe his mum was right. Maybe one day it *would* be their turn. But only then would Luke believe it. Until that day, he'd find it impossible even to *imagine* that they'd ever escape from the world of gray stone and dark shadows they called home.

Foxglove House loomed ahead. *Foxglove!* As if living in a decaying block of flats wasn't bad enough, it had to have a wildflower name that showed how little the planners had thought about this dump. Luke had looked the flower up in a book once. Foxgloves flourished on heaths and open woodland; they didn't even grow in meadows. To flourish in a meadow, he'd discovered, you had to be something like a dandelion—tough enough to crush everything that got in your way.

Lee Young and Mig Russell jumped him as he shouldered his way through the faded red doors.

Russell pinned Luke by the arms with one strong hand, while Young stood in front of him, smiling with all the warmth of a tiger about to pounce.

"I am pleased with yer, kid," he said. "Very pleased. You

may be crap at keeping your eyes open, but you're good at keeping yer mouth shut."

Luke couldn't have replied if he'd wanted to, not with Mig Russell's other hand clamped tightly over his mouth. If he had said anything it would probably have come out as a squeak. Although he had expected this to happen sooner or later Luke's heart was still pounding like a hammer.

Yes, he had expected it. After all, Young and Russell hadn't built their reputation by *encouraging* people to give evidence against them. A few threats and bruises were often all it took to make sure that potential witnesses either suffered memory loss or found something better to do than turn up at a court.

They hadn't had a chance on the day the 4x4 was done, of course. While the Webb guy had been carted off to Accident and Emergency, Luke had been whisked straight from beneath the collapsing wall to the police interview room. As Young and Russell hadn't been invited in for a similar chat straight afterward, Luke assumed they must have worked out that he'd kept quiet. He was right.

"Yeah, I'm pleased," Young repeated, "for your sake. See, if you was to grass on us, you'd be in big trouble. Hear me? Believe me, kid, I'm not nice to know when I'm angry. Am I, Mig?"

Russell laughed, letting his hand drop from Luke's mouth as if coping with two things at once was too much of a challenge. "No, yer ain't. You're a right—"

"I'm not a grass!" yelled Luke. "I'd never grass on anyone. Especially not you two. I got too much respect."

"Yeah?" said Young. "Know who we are, do yer?"

"Lee Young and Mig Russell?" said Luke. "Everyone in East Med knows who you are."

"Then you'll know the police would just love to get their hands on us. They've got no chance, though. We're too smart. The only chance they've got is if somebody breaks the rules and grasses on us. In case they try yer again, we thought we'd better make sure yer know exactly what'll happen if yer crack. . . ."

At the same moment as Mig Russell's hand clamped itself back over Luke's mouth, Young slid a hand into a pocket. Luke stiffened as he saw it come out, saw the glint of the blade.

Young took a step closer, looking amused, now toying lightly with the knife by flicking it from hand to hand. Luke glanced down—only to see something that, if Russell's paw hadn't been preventing him, might have caused him to give a very disrespectful hoot of disbelief. Young's knife wasn't the vicious weapon he'd expected, the sort that would have impressed a fish gutter. It was red-shafted, with a small white cross. It was a Swiss Army penknife, the kind with an attachment for prying stones out of horses' hooves!

Moments later, Luke was wondering how he could have doubted his hero. Young had laid the cold blade of the knife on his cheekbone. Luke felt the point, sharpened to give the penetrative power of a needle, pricking against the skin beneath his eye. A knife that could cope with trapped stones could make short work of removing an eyeball.

Young's chill voice breathed in Luke's ear. "Yer see, kid, if yer was to crack . . . if yer was to grass"—the knifepoint was given a touch more pressure, making Luke shut his eyes tight—"you'd regret it. Yer wouldn't know yerself the next time yer looked in the mirror. In fact, yer might not even *see* yerself next time yer looked in the mirror. Get me?"

Unable to speak, hardly able to move in Russell's tight grip, Luke jerked his head slightly in what he hoped Young would realize was a nod.

He did. With a slow, threatening slide of the blade down the length of Luke's jawbone, Young lifted the knife away, clicked it shut, and returned it to his pocket. "OK. Let 'im go, Mig."

Luke felt his arms being released and realized that his legs were shaking. He slumped heavily against the silvery metal of the elevator door to support himself.

Seeing this, Young, with the obvious satisfaction he always felt after terrifying somebody who couldn't fight back, became almost chatty.

"Yer hear we torched that 4x4?"

"Yeah," said Luke.

The police had told him before sitting him in front of the mug-shot computer, as if they thought it would put him under a bit more pressure. Jerks. Did they think it would make him feel bad for the running guy? Everybody knew he'd get another car off the insurance.

"It was all we could do," said Young. "Had to get rid of any sign of us being in it, see? Just in case yer had grassed us up. Pity. Could have been a nice earner. Lots of people want one." He sniggered at Russell. "Difficult to nick, ain't they, Mig?"

"Unless yer leave 'em unlocked like that idiot," honked his mate.

Maybe it was the relief Luke felt at not having one of his own eyeballs staring up at him from the floor. Maybe it was because he wanted to impress them or because he felt he had to prove, really prove, that he was on their side. Whatever the reason, the words just slipped out.

"He didn't leave it unlocked," said Luke quickly. "I broke in."

Young winked at Russell. "Yeah? How'd yer do that, kid? Smash the window, then fit a new one quick? 'Cos they weren't busted when we got there."

"I picked the lock."

"Yer what?" snorted Young, still amused. "No way. The locks on them 4x4s are a different class."

"I did. Honest."

Russell, taking his lead from Young, leaned casually against the wall instead of giving way to his natural inclination to shut this mouthy kid up with the toe of his boot.

"You're talking turds, kid," he said. "Lee knows. He's an expert. Them 4x4s are as hard to get into as . . ." Finding himself struggling for a comparison, he took the easy way out. ". . . as anything. So just shut your face, eh?"

It was good advice, and one day Luke would regret not taking it. But now, right now, he could only see a way of impressing his heroes.

"I did! I can pick locks. It's easy."

Young's smile had faded. He could put up with macho lies, but only if they weren't pushed too far. Pushing them too far showed a lack of respect. Out came the knife once more. "Prove it, then," he said.

Luke swallowed hard. "I—haven't got what I need," he stammered.

"What's that, then?" said Mig Russell. He wasn't leaning against the wall anymore. Clenching his powerful fists, he'd taken a step closer.

"The tool I use," said Luke. "I—I've just come back from court. I couldn't take it in there with me, could I? It's upstairs."

"What sort of tool?" asked Young. He was toying with his knife, pulling its various attachments in and out.

Luke was sweating now. "It's difficult to describe. It's a thin blade. A bit like . . . that!"

Out of the Swiss Army knife, Young had pried just the thing. What the hell Swiss soldiers used it for Luke didn't know. It wasn't perfect, but the slim blade was good enough.

He reached out a hand. "Can I use your knife?"

Young's face clouded over with suspicion. "What for?"

"To prove it to you," said Luke. "I'll get into that."

To the side of the sliding elevator doors was a small closet set into the wall. Behind it were the controls that the engineer used to reset the elevator mechanism whenever he could be bothered to turn up and do it. The closet had a lock. Nothing complicated. It would be easy.

And so it proved. With Young and Russell leaning close, just in case he was crazy enough to try anything, Luke slid the knife blade into the keyhole. He shut his eyes, feeling the blade become an extension of his fingers, twisting it gently, turning it back and forth as he felt for the pins . . . until, with a dull click, the panel swung open.

"See. Told you, didn't I?"

Luke grinned in triumph. He'd knocked them out. Young's eyes had widened and Russell had his mouth hanging open. Luke eased the blade into its clasp and handed it back.

"Very impressive, kid," said Young. "And yer reckon you can do that for any lock? Fast as that?"

"Not any lock, no," said Luke. "Some are pigs. Most of 'em, though."

Young exchanged glances with Russell. Then, giving a quick jerk of his head to show his pal that it was exit time, he turned to go. His parting words gave Luke a chill down his spine.

"You could be useful to me, kid. *Very* useful. See yer around."

5

VIV DEFOE'S AGED BLUE CAR WAS WAITING FOR LUKE ON a corner, two streets away from the school gates. Luke was well aware that his probation officer—he still thought of him by that title, even though Viv was now tagged "youth offending team operative" or something equally cruddy— had chosen the rendezvous spot with care. Not so close to school as to make Luke feel he was being spied on, but near enough to ensure that he couldn't use the meeting as an excuse for sliding out of school early.

"Nice to see you again, Luke," said Viv, swinging open the passenger door.

Luke climbed in and, after a couple of attempts, managed to shut the ill-fitting door. "When you going to get a new car, Viv?" he asked.

"When you stop breaking into them," said Viv. He smiled as he said it, though, putting Luke at ease.

Viv Defoe was that sort of man. Big and muscular, nobody would want to mix it with him. He could have been the top man on the walkways of any estate he chose. Rumor was that he'd once been just that, up Manchester way. Luke had never had the nerve to ask him outright if it was so.

True or not, nowadays it couldn't have been less likely. Viv was as straight as they came. He didn't wear a uniform, didn't wave a badge, but all the kids knew where he stood. Most of them had sat through one of his frequent school visits, heard him talk about teen crime and the like. As with Luke today, more than a few of them had also met Viv on official business after a trip to court. They all knew the man didn't mess around, didn't pull punches, but neither did he make you feel like you were something that had been scraped off the pavement.

"Glad I got you again," said Luke. "Had old Hopalong last time. Nearly died of mint poisoning every time I met him."

The corners of Viv's mouth twitched, but he didn't rise to the bait. "Mr. Hopgood has recently given up smoking. The mints help him." He glanced at Luke. "Maybe you should try them. See if they help you give up thieving."

Luke felt the color rush to his face. For some reason, getting a slap-down from Viv, even a gentle one like that, felt worse than a whole tutorial's roasting from Mr. Harmer.

"I've tried, Viv. It's just . . ." Luke shrugged. "I dunno. I can't explain it. Maybe it runs in the family, eh?"

"Maybe," said Viv. "There's no law that says it has to, though."

"Suppose not." Luke laughed. "You reckon sucking mints will help, then?"

"No," said Viv seriously. "But I'm hoping this visit might be the start of something that will. You did the right thing agreeing to do it."

No longer quite so sure about that, Luke shut up. He settled for looking out of the windshield at where they were headed. Viv had been carefully threading the car through the back streets of East Med toward the expressway. That was no surprise. Luke hadn't thought for a minute that Mr. Webb, 4x4 owner and flashy-shoes wearer, slummed it in his part of the world. The Webbs were Townies—had to be.

So it came as something of a surprise when Viv didn't turn off the expressway at the Town junction but drove on.

"Where we going, then?" asked Luke, trying to sound casual.

"Rigby Road," said Viv.

"Rigby? . . ." echoed Luke. If there was a road in the area that figured more often in the local news than Rigby Road, then Luke hadn't heard of it. He wouldn't want to, either. The place had the reputation of a war zone. "In West Med?" he asked unnecessarily.

West Med—a mirror estate to East Med, the pair of them thrown up at around the same time on either side of the industrial area that was now buried beneath the glittering Riverside complex. Identical twins at birth, with the difference that whereas East was slowly being given a face-lift, West hadn't even gotten a date for surgery to begin.

"Yes, in West Med," confirmed Viv. "Surprised?"

"Yeah. I mean, with that 4x4 I thought they'd be . . ."

"Townies, right? Plenty of money? No, Luke. They take their daughter, Jodi, to a lot of places." He patted his car's worn and chipped dashboard. "So they didn't want to take chances with an old heap like this. They got into debt—a lot of debt—for something a lot newer and more reliable."

And you helped take it away from them. Viv didn't say

it—that wasn't his way—but Luke suspected that it was what he was thinking. Clever, trying to make him feel guilty. It hadn't worked.

"So? They've probably got an even better one with the insurance money."

That was the way it worked, everybody knew that. He'd heard of people claiming the insurance for stolen televisions they'd actually taken to the dump and ruined carpets that had been, accidentally on purpose, sloshed with paint.

"Don't bank on it," replied Viv. "Unless they can find even more money, they may not have a car at all."

Luke couldn't work that out at all. "How come?"

"Insurance only pays out for what the car is worth at the time of an accident, or when it's stolen. Mr. Webb won't get back as much money as he spent buying the car brand-new. What if they can't find as good a one for the money they get? They'll have to borrow more. And you can be certain that Mr. Webb will have lost his no-claims bonus. Not many people pay the extra it costs to protect it. Whatever car he gets, it'll probably cost him far more to insure it."

"That's not fair," said Luke.

"Wrong. It's perfectly fair. Insurance companies can't pay out more money than they take in. They're businesses—they have to make money. Either they charge the Webbs more or they add a bit on to every car owner's bill. They usually do a bit of both. Every car that gets done costs me money as well. Now *that's* unfair!"

They'd reached the West Med turnoff, a road leading down to a traffic circle. Viv knew which exit to take, which was just as well, because the direction sign was covered by a tattered white sheet carrying the roughly painted message: *Darren Byars, 6 today!*

Good for Darren, whoever he is, thought Luke. Bet he's getting ready to stuff himself with birthday treats, not feeling like his stomach's being slowly filled with cement.

To his dismay, that was exactly how Luke was feeling. Until now, he'd been fine, no problem. The Webb family had been names, no more. Even hearing that the girl was blind hadn't made that much difference. OK, it had made him feel a bit sorry for her. Not being able to watch TV couldn't be much fun. But the Webb family were still just names, not people he knew. It was now sinking in that this was about to change.

Rigby Road was shaped like a large crescent. The houses were terraced, tired-looking. None had garages. Viv brought the car to a halt outside one that looked no different from the rest except that its small postage stamp of a front garden had been concreted over to make a parking spot. The space was empty.

Mrs. Webb was slightly built, neatly dressed, her hair drawn back. She opened the door before Viv's pointed finger had even reached the doorbell. Her speed didn't seem to be matched by enthusiasm, though.

"Come in," was all she said.

They stepped inside. Viv received an uncertain smile, Luke an anxious glance. It didn't help his nerves. Mrs. Webb closed the door gently, then, without another word, led them down the short hallway. Luke heard the pounding beat of loud music coming from upstairs. It matched the thumping of his heart.

Following Viv and Mrs. Webb, Luke found himself in a small living room. Different features registered in an instant: the small, square dining table, laid with an unsuccessful game of solitaire; a bookcase, pushed as far into the corner as it would go; the uncluttered floor. Then, to his right, the pair of faded armchairs placed opposite a matching, and equally faded, sofa. And finally, the unnerving sight of the man stretched out on it; the man he'd last seen—and heard—being loaded into an ambulance.

"Excuse me for not getting up," growled Mr. Webb. "Much as I'd like to, I can't *quite* manage it. Thanks to our young friend, here."

Viv didn't respond, just asked if they could sit down. Still silent, Mrs. Webb waved a hand at the pair of armchairs. Viv took one, indicating to Luke that he should take the other. Mrs. Webb brought a dining chair across for herself.

"Let's get on with it, then," snapped Mr. Webb. He was clearly in a foul mood. Viv seemed not to have noticed.

"I would prefer to wait for Jodi," he said calmly.

"She'll be down soon. She's got some studying to finish off. Not every kid round here spends their time raking the streets."

Luke could feel Mr. Webb's eyes searching for his, like a boxer before a fight. No chance, man. Luke kept his head down, focusing on a spot in the carpet that was wearing thin.

Beside him, Viv was shuffling a notebook onto his knees

and taking out a pen. "Well . . . maybe we can get started on some of the basics, then. As you're aware—and as Luke is aware—this meeting gives him the opportunity to apologize to you all in person—"

"Bit late for that, isn't it!" snapped Mr. Webb.

"Mr. Webb, please. I know this is difficult for you, but believe me, it isn't easy for Luke, either. Like you, he needn't have agreed to this meeting."

Webb was clearly unimpressed. "It was this or be shut away, wasn't it? He's just taken the softer option."

"The softer option? I'm not so sure about that, Mr. Webb. And if Luke thinks the same, then he might be in for a nasty surprise. So, if I can continue . . . "

Viv's voice sounded to Luke like calmness itself, as if preventing a young offender's head from being ripped off was all in a day's work. He'd stopped Mr. Webb's tirade for a while, anyway. But the bad news was that Viv had now turned to him.

"Luke, maybe you'd like to say something."

Say something? The only thing Luke wanted to say was that he didn't want to say a word, nothing, not now, not ever. But he'd always known that was a nonstarter. Time for him to trot out his prepared speech, then, trying to sound sincere and hoping that old man Webb would let him get to the end without landing him one with his plastered leg.

"Er . . . I want to say I'm sorry I got into your car . . . I know it was wrong and I'm never going to do it again . . . I never meant for it to get nicked. . . ."

Short though his little speech had been, throughout it Mr.

Webb had acted like a volcano trying to cap itself. Finally he could hold his anger in no longer.

"But it did, didn't it! Burned out! We've got no car. And my wife can't drive, so *none* of us can get around!" Mr. Webb jabbed a furious finger toward Luke. "All because of him!"

"Luke didn't steal your car, Mr. Webb—" began Viv. He didn't get very far.

"No, but the police told me on the quiet that they reckon he knows who did. He just won't say. Why? Because either he's in with them or he's too scared!"

Luke risked a glance. Mr. Webb looked ready to spit blood—and Luke couldn't really blame him. To Luke's surprise, though, Viv had put his pen away and was rising to his feet.

"Mr. Webb, Mrs. Webb . . ." The probation officer turned toward Mrs. Webb, even though she still hadn't said a word. "I think I should stop this meeting right now. With respect, you don't seem to be approaching it in the right way."

"And what way is that?" asked Mrs. Webb, making her first contribution in a voice shaky with emotion. Unlike her husband, though, she really seemed to want to know the answer.

Remaining on his feet, Viv said, "The court has imposed an action-plan order on Luke. Part of that means that he has to work in his own time to help make good some of the damage he's caused."

Wincing with the discomfort, Mr. Webb levered himself upright on the sofa. "Oh, yes? Miracle worker, is he? Going to lay his hands on my leg and fix it, is he?"

"Allan," said Mrs. Webb, "keep your voice down!"

Luke was vaguely aware that the dull background thump coming from above them had ceased. End of a track, maybe. Whatever, Mrs. Webb was getting to her feet, smiling in a faintly embarrassed way at Viv. "I don't think this is a good idea, Mr. Defoe. I think we all made a mistake."

"That's quite obvious," said Viv.

The probation officer was annoyed, too, Luke could tell, though he also knew that there was no chance of him losing his temper. That wasn't Viv's way.

"I will have to report your change of heart to the court, of course," Viv was now saying. "That's not a problem. It's your right. You were the victims of this crime and nobody is forgetting that. But what I'd like to know is—why? Why write that letter if you feel the way you do?"

Mr. and Mrs. Webb glanced at each other, as if neither wanted to be the one to speak. In any event, the job was done for them.

"Because I talked them into it," said a girl's voice. "It was my idea."

Until that moment, Luke had stuck firmly to his plan to keep his head well down. It dissolved the moment Jodi Webb came into the room.

Ever since being told by Mrs. Mousse, the magistrate, that Jodi Webb was totally blind—as if that made his crime even worse—Luke had been wondering why he hadn't spotted that fact for himself, there in the garage.

He'd been fooled by her appearance, he'd concluded. Blind people were supposed to carry white sticks and wear dark glasses, weren't they? She hadn't had either of them. Blind people should look blind, not normal.

Now, as she came in, Luke couldn't help staring at Jodi Webb to check for the evidence.

He certainly didn't find any in the way she was dressed. With a black T-shirt, boot-cut trousers, and a light denim studded jacket, Jodi looked no different from any other teenage girl. More than that, even. She was better-looking than plenty he could name.

To Luke's even greater surprise, Jodi's eyes didn't give anything away, either. He'd assumed he must have missed something in the garage panic. Close up, he'd expected them to be . . . well, different—turned upward so that only the whites were showing, something like that. But they weren't. Her eyes were clear and colored the deepest brown, just like his own. Only the fact that they tended to stay still as she talked, rather than flicking from side to side, suggested that something wasn't quite right.

Mrs. Webb was the first to react to her daughter's sudden arrival. She stepped forward, helping hands at the ready. But Jodi asked quickly, "Any room next to you, Dad?" and kept on moving confidently toward the sofa. No hesitations, no uncertainty.

Mr. Webb's mood seemed to have softened as quickly as a block of ice cream left out in the sun. Moving his rigid leg to one side, he smiled as he took Jodi's hand and guided her down to the space he'd made.

"Thank you," said Jodi, but with an unmistakeable chill in her voice. "So, what's the problem?" she asked curtly.

Mr. Webb sighed. "Jodi. We—your mum and me—well, we've been talking and . . . look, we don't think this is going to work. . . ."

"We don't think it's"—Mrs. Webb stopped, glancing at Luke as she searched for the right word—"safe." She turned to Viv. "I'm sorry, Mr. Defoe, but . . . what do we know about this boy?"

"Apart from the fact that he's a thief," said Mr. Webb bluntly.

Jodi Webb answered the question for them. "We know he's a good runner, Dad. You said so yourself. You said you could hardly keep up with him."

A good runner? Luke almost burst out laughing. What did that have to do with anything?

"Yes, but . . ." began Mr. Webb.

"Dad, we've been through all this. You and Mum agreed. I know you both think it's risky. I know you think Luke will let me down. You might be right. But he did get me out of the way of that car, and I think that shows something. I think it shows Luke can be trusted."

During this little speech, Jodi had turned to face Luke. He found that scary. Even though he hadn't uttered a word since she'd entered the room, Jodi had still managed to work out where he was sitting. OK, so it couldn't have been that hard, given the small number of available seats, but it was still scary.

Now she was asking him directly, "Am I right, Luke? Can I trust you?"

Trust him? It was the hardest question that Luke had ever

had to answer in his life. Nobody had ever asked him that before.

But this girl was different. He could tell that already. She was calm where her dad was furious, assured where her mum was anxious, friendly when, let's face it, she had no cause to be.

"Well? Can I?"

She wasn't going to let him get away with ducking the question, either. Hesitantly, he found himself nodding, only to realize that she couldn't see him doing it. "Yeah," he mumbled, "yeah, you can."

But—trust him to do what?

Mr. and Mrs. Webb glanced at each other again, shrugging as if they knew when they were beaten.

"Mr. Defoe . . ." began Mr. Webb.

"Viv, please. That's what everybody calls me."

"Viv . . . I'm sorry for . . . for what I said earlier. Jodi's right. We did agree."

With a sigh, Mrs. Webb backed him up. "Yes, we did. We owe it to her to give this scheme a try."

Back to Mr. Webb, like it was a tennis match. "So can we start again? Talk this through?"

Slowly, Viv uncapped his pen again. He laid his notepad back across his knees. But when—finally—he spoke, it wasn't to the Webbs but to Luke.

"What do you think, Luke? Are you willing to continue the meeting? See if we can agree on an action plan for you?"

What did *he* think? What Luke thought was that it didn't sound good. What he thought was that anything requiring him to be in the same county as Mr. Olympic-runner Webb sounded totally crappy, in fact. But what choice did he have? A four-month stretch in Markham sounded even crappier. And besides, what had he just told the girl? Yes, you can trust me.

"If you like." He shrugged. "I don't know what I've got to do yet, anyway."

"Different things," said Jodi with a smile. "But mostly what you're good at. Running."

"Running?" echoed Luke.

Frowning, Viv looked to Mr. Webb for an explanation. "Your letter spoke about Luke working with the visually impaired community. . . ."

"You still don't get it, do you?" said Jodi, answering for her father. She was laughing now, as if she'd reached the punch line of a really good joke. "Those running shoes you tried to steal from our car, Luke—they were mine."

6

"YOURS?" LUKE COULDN'T KEEP THE DISBELIEF OUT OF his voice.

"Yes, mine," said Jodi, now serious. "Blind kids are allowed to have fun as well, y'know."

Luke backpedaled. "I didn't mean . . ."

Jodi stopped him. "Yeah, yeah, I know. You didn't mean we're not allowed to have fun. We can listen to pop music and even follow the same TV shows as everybody else, but sports—oh, no. Not safe."

On the other side of the room, Mrs. Webb stiffened visibly, making Luke think that Jodi's words weren't just aimed at him.

"So what sports do you do, then?" he asked.

Mr. Webb answered, his distaste toward Luke mixed with undisguised pride in his daughter. "You name it. Jodi's tried everything. There's no B1 like her."

"Bee one?" Viv frowned.

"Disability grading system," answered Mr. Webb. "It's used with sports events to ensure nobody gets an unfair advantage. With the visually impaired there are three categories. B2 and B3 athletes have some sight . . ."

"And B1s have none," said Jodi matter-of-factly. "We can't see a dicky bird—or anything else for that matter."

57

"I'm sorry," said Viv.

"Don't be," said Jodi. "It hasn't stopped me from trying archery, cricket, football, judo, goalball, swimming, ten-pin bowling. . . ." Her smile was back. "How's that, Luke? Surprised?"

"Yeah," said Luke. "I didn't know they had . . . you could . . ."

"You didn't know people without good eyesight could do those things? Why not? Why shouldn't I be able to have a go at archery? All I need is somebody to tell me where the target is, then get out of the way! I fire off an arrow, they tell me how close it was to the bull's-eye, and I change my aim for the next one."

What she was saying suddenly struck Luke with force. "You mean . . . you can see the target in your head?" Just like he could see the inside of a lock when he was picking it.

"Ten out of ten." Jodi laughed. "That's exactly the way it is. Some things are harder than others. You want to try playing cards with your eyes closed!"

Luke remembered the game of solitaire laid out on the table. She'd been playing it? But—how?

"I'll give you a game sometime," said Jodi, as if she could read his mind. She laughed again. "Better still, you could be my partner at an ACB rave. Sneak a look at what the others have got in their hands. We'd win every time!"

"ACB rave?" echoed Viv.

"It's a regular event run by the local Association for the Care of the Blind," explained Mrs. Webb. "We use a couple of function rooms at the leisure center. Helping out there is one of the things Jodi—we—had thought Luke could do."

"Not exactly a rave, then." Viv smiled.

"Don't you believe it!" retorted Jodi. "There's one coming up when we take over a sports hall as well. Games in the afternoon, clubbing in the evening. Know the latest moves, do you, Luke?"

"I don't dance," said Luke abruptly.

"So what *do* you do?" asked Mr. Webb. Apart from breaking into cars, he might as well have added.

Luke shrugged. "Nothing much. Hang out round the estate. Watch TV." Even as he said it, he knew that his activities sounded pathetic compared to Jodi's.

"No sports?"

"Not much. There's a basketball hoop near us, but it's usually all bent up because kids swing on it."

"No running?" asked Jodi.

"Only when we do it in games at school." And when I'm there, he thought.

Viv Defoe now seemed much happier with the way the conversation was going. The probation officer had been making a few notes on his pad that Luke hadn't been able to decipher, even though he'd tried. Now, though, Viv scribbled an underlined heading that would have been large enough for Luke to read from the other side of the room: ACTION PLAN.

"Can we talk about exactly what you thought Luke might do? I'm sure I don't need to remind you that my responsibility is to make sure he follows an action plan that will do him some good as well as serving you and the community."

Reparation and rehabilitation, droned a magistrate-style voice in Luke's head. *Reparation means helping the very people your crime affected; rehabilitation means learning the error of your ways so that you will be less likely to offend in the future.* Words, words. Yawn, yawn.

"Now, you mentioned helping at the, er . . . ACB raves." Viv smiled. "That sounded great. Anything else?"

"The blind athletes group," said Mr. Webb flatly.

Viv made a note. "Fine. Anything specific in mind?"

It was Jodi who answered that question. "Very specific. I want Luke to be my guide runner in the London Marathon."

The statement had been made in such a matter-of-fact way that it took a good few seconds for Luke—and Viv, too, judging from the way his pen had stopped moving—to take it in. Even then, Luke wasn't sure he'd heard right.

"The London Marathon?" echoed Luke.

"That's the one. Takes place every April in a place called, er . . . London. Heard of it?"

"What—London or the marathon?" retorted Luke, stung by the sarcasm.

"The race."

"Of course I've heard of it. Seen it on TV, haven't I?"

"Then you're one up on me!" Jodi laughed. "But I've listened to the commentaries and all the other stuff that goes on. It sounds like it's a fantastic race to run in. Big crowds, loads of cheering . . ." In a mercurial moment, her happy mood switched to one of total determination. ". . . And I'm not going to miss out on it."

"You still may have to, love," said Mrs. Webb softly, making one of her rare contributions.

"I am not, Mum! I got through the borough trial. I won my place fair and square, and I'm not going to let them down. I want to run!"

At his end of the sofa, Mr. Webb eased himself into a more comfortable position. He winced, but in a way that suggested it wasn't only his broken leg that was giving him trouble. The whole topic of conversation rankled him.

"Jodi isn't talking about the complete London Marathon, of course," Mr. Webb said. "You have to be over eighteen to take part in that. But they have age-group races for under-eighteens. They're run over the last part of the course, from near Southwark Bridge to the finishing line in the Mall."

"About two and a half miles," added Jodi.

Mr. Webb looked sourly at Luke. "Run that far, can you?"

Luke shrugged. "Reckon so. Never tried it."

"Then you've never tried running it in twenty minutes, either, which is what Jodi is capable of. And she'd manage it if I was able to be with her!" spat Mr. Webb.

Yet again, Viv Defoe stepped in to try and defuse things. "I take it you're usually Jodi's guide runner, Mr. Webb?"

"I was, yes. Have been since she started running. Guided her in the trials. Helped her become the first blind runner to win a place in a mixed borough team." He gestured furiously at his leg. "Not much use to her now, though, am I?"

"But—excuse me if I'm being slow here—aren't there other guide runners you could call on?" Viv asked.

"There are," said Mr. Webb, "but the London Marathon

is a big event. Guides are good runners, they have to be. Most of them are taking part in the race themselves. Those that are left—"

"Aren't fast enough," interrupted Jodi. "The fact that Luke stayed in front of Dad for so long tells me Luke is."

"In other words," said Mr. Webb, jerking a thumb toward Luke, "it's him or no one."

Beside him, Luke sensed Viv stiffen. The probation officer certainly didn't approve of what Luke had done, but Luke knew that part of his job was to protect him against being bad-mouthed. This time it was Jodi who rescued the situation.

"Dad means that if I don't have a guide runner, I'll have to give up my place—don't you, Dad?"

Mr. Webb gave a curt nod. "And the rest. The London Marathon is a big fund-raiser as well as a race. We've already signed up over a thousand pounds of sponsorship. Money that'll help the ACB's work. If Jodi doesn't run, it all disappears." He couldn't resist one final swipe at Luke. "Yet *another* result of your little performance!"

A busted leg. A burned-out car. A grand of sponsorship money gone up in smoke as well. The girl's dream snuffed out. And all because he'd tried to nick a pair of running shoes?

For the first time in his life, Luke felt a real pang of remorse. It helped explain why, when Viv turned to him and asked what he thought of the idea, he agreed so quickly. Well, that and the certain knowledge that he'd have to run a damn sight faster to get away from the hard nuts in Markham.

"All right," said Luke. "When is this London Marathon?"

"Just under two months away," said Jodi instantly, as if she could see the calendar in her head as well. "Sunday, the fourteenth of April."

Luke grimaced to himself. Perfect timing. The last day of the court order. The next morning he could be checking in for Markham.

Luke swept the thought away by risking a joke. "Sunday the fourteenth? Should be OK. I don't think I've got anything on that day." It was a bad move. Mr. Webb was on him in a flash.

"That *day*? If you think you're just going to stroll up that day, then you're wrong! Jodi's athletics club meets on Tuesday evenings and Saturday mornings. And *you* have to be there with her every time, without fail!" He put his hand on Jodi's arm. "It's not going to work, love. I don't think he's got a clue what's involved."

"Then I'll have to spell it out for him, won't I, Dad?" Jodi smiled, oversweetly.

She may have had no expression in her eyes, but her tone of voice told Luke that there was something going on here that was about more than running in some race.

Jodi rose confidently to her feet. "How about if I take Luke out in the garden? See if he can get me all the way round without my breaking a leg." She burst into a sudden giggle. "Sorry, Dad! I didn't mean it!"

Viv was trying not to smile. "Good idea. It will give me a chance to discuss some other details with your parents. Times and places, where Luke has to be and when . . ."

Luke got to his feet, but then had to do no more than fol-

63

low Jodi across the room to the small back door. Apart from extending her hands in front of her so that she didn't smack into the glass, she looked totally at ease. She opened the door, waited for Luke to follow her out, then shut it again. Only then did she feel for his elbow.

"'Scuse fingers," she said, "and 'scuse my parents. They're pains, I know. They mean well, but that's not always enough. If it's any consolation, they're a pain to me as well."

She didn't give Luke a chance to ask why or how. Continuing to hold his elbow in the palm of her hand, she pushed him forward slightly.

"Right, this is how it works. You should always be slightly in front of me. That way, if you forget to tell me what's ahead—like a tiger or a banana skin—it won't matter."

"Why not?"

"Because I'll be hanging on to you, dummy. When you swerve round the banana skin, I'll follow."

"How about the tiger?"

"I'll follow you even faster, won't I!" She poked him in the arm with the index finger of her free hand. "Come on, then, get moving."

It was the strangest feeling, having somebody holding on to him and knowing that she was depending on him to lead her. More than that, depending on him to lead her *safely*. Gingerly, Luke took a few slow paces forward. He was rewarded with a hoot in his ear.

"Blimey, I'd do better hanging on to a snail! A bit quicker, eh?"

"What if you can't keep up?"

"Then I'll tell you to slow down. Just don't be nervous about it, that's all. That's the one thing that'll get me worried."

The garden had a concrete path running from the back door down to a high wooden fence—a distance of about thirty feet at most. Trying to walk at a steady speed, Luke led Jodi to the end of the path.

"Better," she said. "Now back again."

Luke turned on his heel, trying not to stray from the narrow path, only to find that Jodi had let go of his elbow and was now facing him. She was shaking her head, but smiling.

"What do you want, me to lead *you* now?" She reached out, gripped Luke's arms, and turned him back toward the fence. She took his elbow again. "Have another go. Imagine you're a car and I'm a trailer. If you turn too fast you'll bang into me coming the other way! Take it smoothly and I can follow you."

Luke tried again, this time turning in a small semicircle. It worked beautifully. Jodi stayed with him and they headed back down the path. They'd got halfway when she asked him to stop.

"How are my primroses coming along?" she said. "Are the flowers fading yet?"

Luke looked down at the narrow bed of earth between the path and the low side fence. All along it, various unidentifiable shoots were barely poking out of the earth and other equally unrecognizable shrubs had gotten no further than producing a few green buds. There was only one patch of healthy, flowering growth in the whole bed—and Jodi had stopped him at the exact spot.

"Not yet, no," said Luke thoughtfully.

Jodi laughed again. "You're wondering how I knew where they were, aren't you?"

"Maybe."

"Back door to back fence is fifteen paces. Back fence to camellia bush, three paces. Back fence to dogwood, five paces. Back fence to primrose patch, seven paces. You get to remember things when you can't see them."

Luke suddenly felt a flare of anger. She was toying with him. Messing him about. Making him feel sorry for her. "So what d'you need me for, then?" he snapped.

He realized what a dumb question it was the moment he'd asked it. Of course there was a big difference between finding your way around a small back garden and finding your way around outside. And a world of difference between that and trying to run in a crowded, jostling race through the streets of London. Even so, the reply Jodi gave him was unexpected.

"Simple. You saved me once. I want you to save me again."

"Save you again? From what?"

"Not what. Who. My parents."

Luke glanced back at the house. Through the windows, he could see Mr. and Mrs. Webb, he looking bitter, she looking resigned but anxious, as they thrashed out with Viv the details of this weird arrangement. He remembered Jodi's barbed comments, the comments that he'd suspected weren't being aimed at him. What had he walked into?

"Look, don't get me wrong," said Jodi quietly. "It can't be easy for them. But they're suffocating me. They're too worried to let me go to a normal school, and I refuse to be shut away in a special school. So I don't go to a school at all. . . ."

You and me both, thought Luke.

"Mum teaches me at home. That might be bearable if she didn't want to do just about everything else for me as well." Jodi sighed. "That's why I started playing sports. Just to get out of the house. But that's become a nightmare as well. Dad wants to turn me into the star runner he wasn't good enough to be."

You think you've got problems, Jodi! Luke almost retorted. My mum hasn't got the time or energy to do anything for me. As for my dad, at least yours is still around. . . . Then he looked into her still, unblinking eyes. It brought him sharply to his senses. For a moment, he'd been thinking of Jodi Webb as a normal girl. But she wasn't—she was anything but normal.

"I thought you *wanted* to be a star runner," he said. "That's what this marathon's all about, ain't it?"

Luke suddenly felt his elbow being gripped again, but this time with fierce force as his thinking was battered aside.

"No, it isn't!" snapped Jodi. "It's about me being as normal as I can be. Doing something that every other kid takes for granted. Running. Get that? Being blind means there are some things I can't do. I accepted that a long time ago. But there's no way I'm going to let it stop me from doing the things I *can* do. That's why I run, Luke—because I can! All I'm asking is for you to help me."

She stopped, releasing his elbow as she turned to face him. "Like I helped you."

"Coming up with this scheme to keep me out of Markham?" said Luke.

"Not just that," said Jodi.

"How d'you mean?"

"The two who stole our car. When you pushed me out of the way, one of them laughed, didn't he? And one of them shouted something—something I didn't tell the police."

See yer, Lukey!

"You knew who they were, didn't you?"

Luke stiffened. "I . . . No! They knew who I was, don't ask me how, but I'd never seen them before."

The lie must have sounded convincing. "Really?" said Jodi. "Then I could probably identify them better than you."

"What?"

"When you can't see, you have to work harder on your hearing," she said. "If I heard their voices again, Luke, I'd know them."

⌐

AS LUKE PICKED UP HIS JACKET, HIS MUM, HER EYES RED-rimmed with tiredness, looked up from her ironing board.

"Where are you going?"

"Out."

"I can see that, Luke. I asked where."

"Just out," said Luke. "Don't know where till I get there, do I? Down the green, maybe. See who's around."

Mrs. Reid sighed with the air of a woman who no longer has any energy left for the fight.

"You haven't told me how it went with that family. What was their name—Webb?"

Luke picked up his shoes, without looking at her. "You could have come with me. Like you could have come to the court with me."

"I couldn't."

"You could. I told you when it was, you just didn't listen. You never listen."

"And I tell you to stay out of trouble!" exploded Mrs. Reid. "But do *you* ever listen? No!"

Switching the iron off, she slammed it down into its cradle. The act seemed to flick her own temperature from hot to cool. Laying the now pressed child's dress across the back of a chair, she said more calmly, "What am I supposed to do,

Luke? Leave Billy and Jade on their own? I can't keep asking Mrs. Roberts next door to take them in, and you know I can't afford a babysitter. It's not easy for me, either."

Luke knew that. His brother, Billy, had just turned three, and Jade, his sister, was almost two. From the screaming that went on, it often amazed Luke that they'd survived as long as they had. He regularly felt like shoving the pair of them down the waste chute, so what it was like for his mum having to spend all day, every day, cooped up with them, he couldn't imagine.

Calmer himself now, he tossed his jacket over the back of a chair and sat down. "The visit didn't go too bad," he said. "Better than I thought it would."

"Come on, then, what happened?"

"Well—I found out Jodi Webb's a runner."

"Really? The blind girl?"

"Yeah. She does all sorts."

"But—running?" Mrs. Reid shook her tousled head in amazement.

Luke grinned. "You haven't heard the half of it. Wants to take part in the London Marathon, doesn't she? That's part of my service job—to be her guide run—"

A sudden screech from the kitchen cut him short. Leaving Luke midword, his mum frantically rushed off to sort out the trouble.

It was the same old story. They came first, he came nowhere. Snatching up his jacket again, Luke felt in the pocket for his lock pick. Angrily yanking on his running shoes, he strode to the door.

"I thought we were talking." His mum had reappeared, a sniveling Jade in her arms and a scowling Billy at her side.

"I've finished," snapped Luke. "See you later."

"You still haven't told me where you're going."

"Australia and back."

"Luke—don't get into any trouble. Please!"

Even as she said it, though, his mum was struggling to prevent her two young ones from restarting the fight she'd just broken up.

"Why the hell not?" shouted Luke. "You don't care!"

It was the last straw of a bad day. "Don't you dare speak to me like that!" screamed Mrs. Reid. "I do care! I don't want you ending up like your father!"

But the front door had slammed, and her son was already out of earshot.

AT THE END OF THE WALKWAY, LUKE STOPPED AND GAZED out over the railing. It was dusk, the time when Townie kids were tucked up indoors doing their homework. Not on the East Med Estate, though. Life was different here. Dusk was the time when the kids came out, like creatures of the night.

Far below, he could see them: meeting, clustering, moving on again. Even from that distance, Luke had a good idea who was who. The clues varied. Clothes for one, exaggerated swagger for another. There were those who preferred roaming about in twos and threes and those, like him, who were solo operators. He knew which groups shouted too loudly, suddenly springing into mock fights, and which groups would be on the lookout for the real thing. Yes, Luke knew them all. To him they weren't faceless nothings up to no good—they were real people . . . and his kind.

Sinister? Frightening? That's what adults were always saying. But did those adults think about where else they could go, what else they could do?

These nighttime gatherings weren't sinister or frightening to him, not to any of them. They were more like friendly get-togethers, usually the only one of their day. OK, they might give the owner of the Chinese takeout a bit of lip, break the odd window, lift a few things from people rich enough to own them in the first place, ride around in their cars. But it was just their way of having fun.

That's why people like Lee Young and Mig Russell won so much respect. They did what they wanted, when they wanted. They had more fun than anybody else. They were undisputed leaders. If they noticed you, it made you feel important. If you got on the wrong side of them, it was bad news—but whose fault was that? The rules were clear. Follow them, don't grass, and you'll be all right. Welcome. Join the family.

Hands in pockets, Luke shouldered through the door at the end of the walkway. He was met by the ever-present smell of cats—and total darkness. The bulb on the stairwell landing was gone, either blown, busted, or swiped.

While his eyes became adjusted, he thrust out a hand and began feeling his way along the wall. A difference in surface, from rough to smooth, told him he'd found the elevator door. He could see a bit more now, but not enough to save him from cracking his shin against something hard and metallic. Cursing loudly, he bent down and played his fingers across it. A shopping cart on its side. Mrs. Brixton in the end flat, probably, wheeling her grub home from the supermarket, up in the elevator unloading it, then being neighborly and leaving the cart for somebody else to use—or fracture a shin on.

Shoving it aside, Luke moved slowly forward, feeling for the top stair with an outstretched foot. Finding it, he started down, going carefully until the dim light coming up from the landing below helped him to see where he was going. Only then did the thought strike him.

That's what it must be like for Jodi Webb all the time.

LUKE DIDN'T HEAD INTO THE HEART OF THE ESTATE. For what he had in mind, there was another East Med rule that you ignored at your peril: *Don't steal from your own kind.*

He'd crossed the Bridge and was walking up toward the town center when he saw the squad car coming. Quickly bending down, he pretended to be tying up his shoelace. But they'd seen him. Doing a sharp U-turn, the car drew up alongside. Both officers jumped out, a hard and nasty-looking one from the passenger side and a world-weary version from the driving seat.

"And where are we off to, then?" said Nasty, stepping in front of him.

"Town," said Luke.

"Anywhere special?"

Luke shook his head. "No. Just looking round."

"What for, Luke?" Weary had appeared at his side. "A car to get into?"

The sound of his own name gave Luke a shock. He'd never seen either of these two before. "How d'you know my name?"

Nasty stuck his face close. From the smell of his breath he'd had curry before going on duty. "Luke, you're famous. We all know who you are. Brave Luke Reid, who goes round thieving from blind kids." His tone changed gear, from nasty to nastier. "The kid who's too scared of Lee Young and Mig Russell to rat on them."

Luke sighed. "I didn't see them." He'd said it so often it was becoming easier and easier. "Saw two men, didn't I? That's who it was."

It was Weary's turn now. "Turn out your pockets, please."

"What? Why?"

"Why? I'll tell you why." Weary was smiling now, pretend pleasant. "That 4x4. It hadn't had any of its windows bashed in. The only broken glass they found was out in the road, where the heat of the flames blew the windows out. Not an itty-bitty bit inside. You know what that tells me? It tells me you're a smarter thief than your average thief. You did that lock—and you don't pick locks with your toenails."

"So turn out your pockets," snapped Nasty.

Luke hesitated. If they found his lock pick he was in trouble. Slowly, he dipped into his jeans and jacket pockets. He pulled out a few coins, hoping that would satisfy them. It didn't.

Nasty glanced at Weary. His superior nodded, but with a look that said "Take it easy."

Luke held out his arms while Nasty ran both hands down his sides, pounding them just that bit harder than was necessary to detect anything he'd left in his pockets or tucked inside his shirt. Then the same to his legs, inside and out, as if they suspected he might have a crowbar stitched into the lining of his jeans.

"Nothing," said Nasty, sounding disappointed.

Without a word, Weary sniffed, strolled round the front of the squad car, and climbed back in behind the wheel. Nasty flopped into the passenger seat. He couldn't resist a parting shot through the open window.

"Change your mind about talking and life could become a lot easier, Luke. Until then—we'll be watching you. All the time. Don't forget that."

Luke watched the car cruise away, waiting until it had disappeared from view. Then he turned, heading back over the Bridge to the gray safety of East Med—to where police cars only came when they were called, if then.

He didn't hurry. The lock pick tucked inside his sock was starting to rub, but he didn't want to remove it just in case they really were watching him. You can't trust cops, that's what his dad had always said.

LUKE CLIMBED INTO VIV DEFOE'S NOISY OLD CAR AND
slammed the door hard.

"Got a problem?" asked the probation officer mildly.

"You didn't have to give me a lift. It ain't that far away. I
could have got there on my own."

"I know."

"So why'd you have to come and get me? Everyone on
East Med knows who you are. They'll all know I'm doing
service again."

"You mean they don't know already? I thought news trav-
eled fast around here." He glanced at Luke. "You're telling
me *nobody* has mentioned it?"

Luke didn't reply. He knew what Viv was hinting at; or,
rather, *who* he was hinting at. Lee Young and Mig Russell—
and the likelihood that they'd have paid Luke a call. Luke
switched direction before Viv could push it further.

"I'm only saying you didn't have to come and get me."

"Just trying to be helpful, Luke." Viv smiled. "I knew you
wouldn't want to be late for your first training session. Feeling fit?"

"Fit enough," said Luke.

He was lying. Oh, he was feeling fit enough to jog round
a running track. That wasn't the problem. He was scared.

That was the problem. Viv was a smart one, all right. Luke definitely would have "forgotten" if the probation officer hadn't turned up to get him.

Up till now, his community-service jobs had been a joke. There'd be a group of them, like a chain gang in a film, sponging graffiti, picking up litter or whatever, and giving the do-gooding volunteer in charge so much lip he'd usually let them off early just to get a bit of peace.

But this time was different. This time he was on his own. It was all up to him.

THE PEMBROKE SPORTS COMPLEX SOUNDED GRANDER than it was. Built some fifty years before, it had slowly decayed as people gradually stopped playing sports in favor of sprawling in front of the television to watch others do it. At one stage, with more windows splintered than whole, it had become known locally as the Broke. The name had stuck, even though money had recently been pumped into renovating the place and it now looked quite respectable.

Viv maneuvered his way across the parking lot and stopped in front of the main building. A new sign by the entrance advertised the delights of the squash courts, badminton courts, and fitness center to be found inside. It also mentioned that function rooms were available, reminding Luke that this was where Jodi's "rave" was being held the following weekend.

But it was another sign that gave the tension Luke was already feeling a further twist. It was old and faded, as if it had been attached to the wall when the Broke was first built.

It showed a pointing finger and read: ATHLETICS TRACK.

The refurbishment of the center hadn't extended to the Broke's running-track facilities. Luke had been on it the previous summer, when they'd all been carted out here for a politically correct sports day in which nobody won and nobody lost. He'd placed first in the hundred-meter and been given exactly the same poxy certificate as leaden-legged Aaron Wickes, who'd trailed in last. Great. Maybe they'd do the same with GCSE Math, awarding him an A just for turning up and giving it a try. Would they ever. Anyhow, Luke knew that the pathway round behind the building didn't lead to a sparkling crimson running surface but to a prehistoric cinder track with painted white lines.

But if Luke found the prospect grim, the same couldn't be said for those turning up all around him. Sounds of laughter and welcome filled the air. Sports bags were being unloaded from car trunks by people Luke's age, to be slung across their backs and carried off in the direction of the pointing finger. The only thing that made the scene different from any other youth sports club was that some of the members were being guided to their destination.

"You're here, then," said a voice from behind Luke. It was Mr. Webb, perched uncomfortably on a pair of crutches. "That's something, I suppose."

Viv nodded a welcome. "Evening, Mr. Webb. Where's Jodi?"

Lifting one of his crutches as if it were a broken wing, Mr. Webb pointed over to where Jodi was already being led toward the track by a gray-haired man. "One of the other parents gave us a lift. Mr. Blanchflower. He can't do it every time, though. I'll probably have to sweet-talk somebody else into it next week."

The thought of Mr. Webb sweet-talking anybody was more than Luke's imagination could handle—especially when Jodi's father finally glared directly at him to ask, "Where's your gear? You don't think you're running in what you've got on, I hope."

"Yeah." Luke shrugged, looking down at his T-shirt, jeans, and running shoes. "Why not?"

But Viv was already on his way to the rear of his car. "He's only joking, Mr. Webb," he said, pulling out a duffel bag. He handed it to Luke, muttering, "There's a pair of shorts, a sweatshirt, and a proper pair of running shoes. They should fit."

"Thanks, Viv," said Luke, not sure whether he was grateful or furious. "Thanks a lot."

BY THE TIME LUKE EMERGED FROM THE CHANGING ROOM, Jodi was warming up with the others. He was surprised by the numbers. There must have been at least forty of them, the youngest aged about ten and the oldest about seventeen—inhabitants of a world Luke never knew existed. Under the eye of an exercise leader, the athletes were on the grass oval inside the track, sitting splay-legged as they stretched to touch one toe then the other.

Viv had found other things to do—"I'll be back in time to give you a lift home," he'd said—but Mr. Webb was all too visibly there. He'd parked himself on a bench near the athletes, crutches at his side, his leg stuck out like a thick white log. Catching sight of Luke, he pointed sourly to a space beside Jodi. She turned before he'd even sat down.

"Hi," she said. "Dad told me you'd arrived. He didn't expect you to come. I think you surprised him."

"Yeah?" said Luke. "Well, it hasn't put a smile on his face, that's for sure. So, what's happening?"

"Warm-ups, of course. Stretches, that kind of thing."

"When does the running start?"

"Hello—after we're warmed up. Don't you warm up before you run?"

"Nope," said Luke, dismissively. "Don't often have to run, do I?"

"Maybe it's time you started warming up, then," whispered Jodi with a smile. "You might get away next time."

She swung back to carry on with her routine. Next to her, Luke went through the motions, pretending to do the exercises but not putting the slightest effort into it. He spent more time looking at those around him, trying to work out which were the sighted athletes and which weren't. Sometimes it was obvious. One teenage girl, older than Jodi, was wearing a pair of dark glasses. A ten-year-old boy's eyes, white and upturned, gave him away. But mostly, Luke simply couldn't tell.

Why should he be surprised? What had Jodi said to him in her garden? Running was about her being as normal as she could be. He was starting to understand. She wanted to be accepted for *who* she was, not *what* she was; judged by what she could do rather than what she couldn't.

Luke glanced down at his gear. Viv should have been a tailor. His estimates had been good. Everything fit well, with the running shoes feeling so comfortable Luke had to flex his toes to prove he had them on. He was grateful. He wouldn't have looked like a runner otherwise. Sure, some of them might be wondering *who* he was, but without the clothes he'd have stood out, causing others to wonder *what* he was, why he was there. And at that moment, Luke found himself hoping that as few of them as possible discovered the truth. On the walkways of East Med it was different. Having a record earned you respect. But here . . .

"Hey! Reid!"

The voice, cold and hard, from the wooden bench behind, snapped Luke out of his reverie. The warm-ups had finished. Athletes and guides were getting to their feet, pairing up. Luke's fists clenched automatically. He didn't turn, though, forcing Mr. Webb to shout again.

"Reid! Here!"

Jodi's father was ferreting in a sports bag at his side. This time, slowly and deliberately, Luke wheeled round and walked across to him. "My name's Luke," he said.

If Mr. Webb had heard, he didn't let it show. "You need this," he growled, holding out the short strap he'd retrieved from his bag.

Luke didn't reach out to take it, just repeated, "My name's Luke."

This time Mr. Webb did react. Stone-faced, he thrust an arm over each of his crutches and hauled himself to his feet.

"I know what your name is, thief," he hissed in Luke's face. "It's on every letter I've had from the magistrates' court. Now take this and get back to my daughter."

The strap had loops at each end. Jodi took one the moment Luke arrived back at her side, pushing her right wrist through the loop.

"You put your left wrist through the other end," she said.

Luke did so. The strap was just long enough to give them both the room they needed to pump their arms while running. It didn't take a genius to work out that he would be using it to guide Jodi round the track.

"Ready, then?" he asked.

"Not yet," said Jodi. "Watch the other runners for a minute."

"What for? To see who's your biggest challenger?"

Jodi laughed. "Luke, you need to check out the other guide runners. See what they do."

Kicking himself yet again for being so dumb, Luke turned his attention to what was happening on the track. The blind athletes and their guides were beginning to jog round—some at a leisurely pace, others at a speed that surprised him.

But, slow or fast, the pairs all moved smoothly together, with the guides just ahead and to the right of their runners. Something about each pair struck Luke as unusual, though. He just couldn't work out what it was.

"Take me across to the fifteen-hundred meters start," said Jodi after a couple of minutes.

"Where?"

"It's in the back straight. Just after the first bend. It's a good place to start."

She took his elbow, just as she had in her garden, holding it gently as he steered her across the grass to where a couple of other runners and their guides were getting ready to set off. Luke could almost feel Mr. Webb's eyes burning into his back at every step.

"Stop," said Jodi, when they were just a couple of meters away.

Again, Luke wondered how she'd managed to judge where they were. Surely she hadn't paced out the whole area and committed it to memory!

She hadn't, of course. While he'd been concentrating on where they were going, she'd been listening. "Hear that?" she said.

Luke frowned. "Hear what?"

"The guides, of course."

The talking. *That's* what had seemed unusual. The runners he'd seen in races on television had all been striving to bust a gut. Talking had been the last thing on their minds. But here the guides were gabbing on nonstop. As a pair came out of the first bend and sped past them into the back straight he caught a few words.

"Turning . . . straighten now . . . straight . . ."

Jodi tugged at his elbow. "Hear that? Guides don't just have to run. They have to talk all the way round as well."

Luke was starting to realize that this wasn't going to be quite as easy as he'd first thought. "So when do they breathe?"

83

"Dunno." Jodi laughed. "Come on, let's give it a try. I'm sure my dad is waiting to see how big a mess you make of it."

Luke glanced over at the glowering Mr. Webb. "You're not wrong there. He doesn't like me very much, does he?"

"Like you?" said Jodi, serious now. "Luke, he thinks you're the scum of the earth. He hates you."

THEY STARTED AT WHAT LUKE THOUGHT WAS A GENTLE pace. Well, gentle compared to tearing down a slippery back alley with a panting Mr. Webb on his tail.

Jodi was moving easily in the inside lane. Luke ran— jogged, more like—half a pace ahead and just outside her, in the second lane. Between them, the strap flapped loosely as their arms pumped backward and forward.

"How close am I to the edge?" called Jodi.

Luke glanced down and to his left at the raised concrete rim that divided the running track from the grass oval. "Really close."

"Move out a bit, then. Don't let me get near enough to tread on it. Not unless you want to carry me the rest of the way round with a sprained ankle."

"And deliver you to your dad? No, thanks."

Still running smoothly, Luke moved out slightly. The strap tightened for a moment, then loosened again as Jodi followed him out.

"That edge is just about the only thing you'll have to watch out for here. The mini-marathon's going to be a lot harder."

84

"Don't see why," replied Luke, only half joking. "Curbs are bigger, ain't they? Easier to spot."

"Because, dummy, you won't just have to be on the lookout for curbs. There'll be cracks in the road, traffic islands, overhanging branches, refreshment tables, race marshals—"

"All right! I hear you!"

He had, too. And not only because of Jodi's list, which he didn't doubt could have grown a lot longer if he hadn't stopped her. They were approaching the bend at the far end of the track. Worse still . . .

"Listen," he shouted, failing to keep the rising panic out of his voice, "we're coming up to the bend. And there's somebody in the way."

Although they were only moving at a jogging pace, Luke's wrist still received a nasty wrench as Jodi stopped dead and the strap dragged him to a halt as well.

"What's the problem?"

"Luke, do me a favor. Don't say things like that."

"Like what?"

"Like, 'we're coming up to a bend,' or, 'there's somebody in the way.' Unless you want to really wind me up, I don't want to know."

Luke couldn't understand it. He thought he'd been doing the right thing. "What do you want to know, then?"

She didn't answer his question directly. Instead she said, "Look, imagine you're me for a minute. Shut your eyes. Done it?"

"Yeah."

"Right. Now—ahead of you there's a post sticking out of

the ground. If you run into it, you're gonna get a whack right where it hurts most. So I say to you, 'Luke! You can't see it, but there's a post sticking out of the ground!' Does that help?"

Luke thought about it. Help? No, it didn't. It made his eyes water to think about it, but that was all. "No," he said.

"Same here. I don't want to know what's in the way, Luke. All I want to know is what I've got to do to avoid it. Move left, move right, slow down—stop dead, if that's what you reckon is best."

"But I thought . . ."

"I'd want to decide for myself? Forget it. When we're running, you're in charge. You make the decisions. I obey them."

Him, in charge? At school they wouldn't have trusted him to take charge of a pencil sharpener. He wasn't sure he could handle this.

"What if I get it wrong?"

"Then we argue about it afterward," said Jodi firmly. "So—you ready to get going again?"

They set off once more, still at not much more than a jogging pace. Approaching the bend, Luke remembered the guide runner Jodi had made him listen to.

"Go left a bit," he called, "we're starting the bend."

"Better," said Jodi.

The bend was curving away to their left, leading into the finishing straight. Still making sure he was half a pace ahead, Luke tried to keep a safe distance between Jodi and himself all the way round.

It was harder than he'd ever thought possible. At one

point, Jodi began turning tightly to the left. Only when he felt the strap tighten did Luke think to shout, "Too much! Straighten up a bit!"

But now Jodi was starting to run toward the outside of the track instead of following the curve of the bend. The strap linking them was flapping completely loose and he had to move out quickly to avoid having Jodi run into him.

"To your left again," he yelled. "Not too much! Perfect!"

They may have been zigzagging like a pair of slow-motion drunks, but they were almost there. Ahead of them was the finishing straight, its white lines stretching away into the distance. "Straighten up!" Luke yelled.

Jodi responded instantly. The strap tightened as Luke moved out to lead her away from the track edge, then loosened again as he moved back into step. Still jogging gently, Luke guided Jodi safely down the straight and across the finish line. Mr. Webb was waiting to meet them, perched vulturelike on his crutches.

"At that speed you wouldn't have won a toddlers' race at a play-school sports day," he said to Jodi.

Jodi was unruffled. "Good thing I'm entered for the London Marathon, then, isn't it!"

"You know what I mean," growled Mr. Webb. He turned to Luke. "She has to take her speed from you. If you're going slow, she has to go slow." His mouth twisted into a sneer. "You can run faster, I assume? Or do you have to have somebody chasing you before that happens?"

"Dad! That's not fair! You know it takes a lot of practice."

Mr. Webb's expression didn't change, neither did his eyes

leave Luke's. "Then you'll both have to practice some more, won't you?"

PRACTICE THEY DID. IT SEEMED AS IF JODI COULDN'T RUN enough. They did four laps, then a fifth, taken at a slightly faster pace each time. Then Luke asked if she wanted to stop. Whether it was the prospect of returning to her misery guts of a father, watching their every move from his bench, or because she was enjoying herself so much, Jodi replied, "One more lap!"

This would make six laps. About a mile and a half. They'd only done them at a crawl, but Luke was starting to feel it. His thighs were tightening and he was breathing heavily.

"You're doing well," said Jodi.

"Thanks," said Luke.

In spite of his aches, Luke grinned. He didn't expect Mr. Webb to agree, but he reckoned he was getting the hang of things. He was talking to Jodi more—maybe that was why he was getting so out of breath. . . . They also seemed to be having fewer zigzag spells, even round the bends.

Jodi happily leaned into a starting position. "On our marks, then . . . get set . . . go!"

This time, they surged off at a good pace. Luke took them around the first bend, Jodi running smoothly inside him and a perfect half step behind. They were so in tune Luke felt his shouts of "Left . . . left" were almost unnecessary.

Into the back straight. A slight wobble coming out of the bend, corrected by his firm call of, "Straighten!"

They were going well. Too well. Another runner and his

guide were directly ahead. They were catching up with them fast. Closer, closer. If Luke and Jodi didn't move out or slow down, they'd run into the back of them.

He glanced at Jodi. What had she said earlier? *When we're running, you're in charge. You make the decisions. I obey them.* Could he believe that? Could she really trust him that much?

They were almost on top of the other runners. Another few strides and they'd hit them. . . .

"Move out!" shouted Luke, moving out quickly himself. He felt the strap tighten. Had Jodi heard? He shouted again, louder, an order almost. "Move out, Jodi!"

The strap loosened. She'd done as he'd said!

"Out, out . . ." continued Luke. They were heading toward the middle of the track now—and drawing level with the other two runners. "Straighten!" he shouted. "We're overtaking!"

Still in stride, they surged forward. Luke, not daring to think about what was happening inside him, settled for what he could see out of the corner of his eye. They were side by side with the other runners—the ten-year-old boy and gray-haired Mr. Blanchflower who'd given the Webbs a lift to the track. Then, slowly, the boy had gone; Luke could only see the bobbing outline of Mr. Blanchflower. Another few paces and he'd disappeared as well—only the sound of pounding feet and Mr. Blanchflower's puffing told Luke that they were still there.

"Yeah, we're past them!" he yelled in delight. "Move in, Jodi!"

"You're learning," Jodi called out, smoothly doing what she'd been told. "I thought I was going to have to stop."

"You what?" said Luke as what she'd said sank in. "You mean you could tell we were catching up to somebody?"

Jodi hooted with laughter. "I'm blind Luke, not deaf! I'd have been able to hear us getting closer to anybody. But that was Mr. Blanchflower we just passed, guiding his grandson, Tom. You can hear him puffing from the other side of the track!"

They were almost on the final bend. Again Luke began guiding Jodi in a curve. Instructions were coming more naturally now, and he was able to concentrate better on keeping in step. That wasn't easy. He wasn't puffing quite as loudly as Mr. Blanchflower, but he was definitely starting to gasp for breath. He'd be pleased to call it a day.

Jodi looked like she could go on running all day, though. Coming out of the bend and into the home straight, she shouted: "You know what, Luke? Every time I come round this bit I imagine it's the final stretch of the London Marathon! I'm in front of Buckingham Palace and the queen's looking down from her balcony and cheering me on!"

Luke realized immediately that the fantasy had given Jodi an extra burst of energy. Instead of being half a step behind, she'd almost drawn level with him. He had to get them back into position, he knew that. Tired as he was, he too had to speed up. Could he manage it?

He could! More than that, he found extra reserves himself, as if Jodi's enthusiasm had spread to him as well. Ahead he could see the finish line beckoning.

"Come on, then!" he yelled. "Pretend it's your marathon! Go for it!"

He stretched out. Jodi followed, the sheer delight of running illuminating her face. Soon they were almost sprinting, racing each other.

As they closed on the line, Luke forgot that he was a guide. He was a runner, a sprinter, going for the win. Gritting his teeth, he pushed himself even harder, not noticing that the strap linking him to Jodi had stretched taut.

Only when she screamed, "Slow down!" did he come to his senses. He slowed instantly. Behind him, almost pulled off her feet, Jodi was struggling to stay upright. Luke's change of pace had helped, however. She was recovering her stride—but, in the panic, Luke had forgotten about the danger of her getting too close to the edge of the track.

Jodi's left foot clipped the concrete strip. If she'd been running steadily it might not have mattered too much. But she was already half stumbling as she tried to slow down. Hitting the edge finished things off. Her legs gave way and, with a cry of shock, she crashed to the cinders. An instant later, as the strap linking them tightened and twisted, Luke found himself being dragged down with her.

Ignoring the fierce pain from his skinned elbow, Luke struggled to his knees. To his relief, Jodi appeared not to be hurt. She'd already released herself from the strap that bound them together and was bouncing back onto her feet, the only evidence of her fall being the gray cinder marks along the side of her left leg.

"Jodi! Jodi!" Mr. Webb was heading their way, roaring

and hopping simultaneously. By the time Luke was back on his feet and standing at Jodi's side, he'd arrived. "Are you all right?"

"I'm fine, Dad," said Jodi quickly. She flexed her left ankle to prove it. "It was my fault. I got carried away."

But Mr. Webb wasn't that easily fooled. "Rubbish!" he spat, turning on Luke. "I saw what happened. That was your fault, Reid."

Luke's fists clenched tight as the temptation to smack Jodi's dad in the mouth became almost overwhelming. What held him back was the touch of her fingers on his, light as a feather and unseen by Mr. Webb, as if to say, "Don't do it. That's what he wants. He's trying to break you."

So he stood his ground and said simply, emphasizing each word, "My name is Luke."

For all the good it did he might just as well have said that his name was Rumpelstiltskin. Mr. Webb raved on. "Your fault," he repeated with venom, jabbing a finger into Luke's chest for good measure. "Just as I expected. You want to know why? Because, Reid, given the chance, I just knew you'd do what comes naturally."

Mr. Webb pointed angrily at the home straight Luke and Jodi had just raced down. "A guide has to think about his runner first, last, and always. Well, you didn't. You weren't running for Jodi, just now. You were running for yourself. Hear me? For yourself!"

He was eyeballing Luke, defying him to look away. "And that's just what you'll always do when it comes to the crunch, isn't it, Reid? Put yourself first."

Until then, Luke had been standing his ground, refusing to be intimidated. Now, without a word, he undid the strap that was still dangling lifelessly from his left wrist and put it into Jodi's hand. Then he turned and left them to it.

He was outside waiting as Viv drew up. "How did it go?" said the probation officer.

"All right."

They were the only words Luke spoke all the way back. He saw no need to go into details. No need to explain why he'd walked away. No need to say that it wasn't just because Jodi's father had angered him.

And, especially, no need to admit that he knew Mr. Webb had been right.

9

JODI SETTLED DOWN IN FRONT OF HER COMPUTER. Reaching forward, she felt for the little raised notches at the bottom of both the F and J keys on its keyboard. With her left index finger on F and her right on J, she knew her other fingers would automatically be in the right positions to cover the other keys. Smoothly and confidently, she began to type:

> I'm lucky to be living in the twenty-first century. I'm able to type this essay into my computer. What's more, although I can't see what I've written, I can read it! At the bottom of my keyboard I've got a device that lets me do just that. It's a modern invention, but only because it's a piece of computer equipment. The idea behind it came from somebody who was born about two hundred years ago. Somebody who definitely changed the world.

That had been the title of the biographical essay Jodi's mum had set as her English assignment: *A Man/Woman Who Changed the World*. Jodi would have loved her subject to have been a female, but the person she admired most had been a man, and there wasn't much she could do about that!

Louis Braille was born in the year 1809. He lived in a little town near Paris. His father was a craftsman who made all sorts of things out of leather. One day, when Louis was three, he found one of his father's tools. It was a tool called an awl. This is a sharp-pointed tool used to make holes in leather. There was an accident. Somehow, Louis stuck the awl into one of his eyes. The wound became infected. Soon, the infection spread to Louis's other eye. He became totally blind.

Louis refused to let his new condition beat him. He won a place at a special school in Paris, the Royal Institute for Blind Youth. There, he was taught useful things—not! Nobody expected much of blind kids. They were only expected to master simple skills. So, Louis was told that if he didn't want to end up begging on the streets, he had to learn how to make a cane chair or sew a pair of slippers. Louis proved them wrong. He became an accomplished musician for a start.

Maybe Louis Braille would have liked to be living in the twenty-first century, thought Jodi. He could have joined a pop group! She might have enjoyed listening to his music at top volume!

Jodi typed on, the words coming easily. She wrote about how the few books in the school's library were huge and unwieldy, with every letter printed extra large and raised off the paper so that it could be felt by the reader's fingertips. She wrote about how Louis's belief that there had to be a better way was confirmed when he heard of an army code system that used raised dots and dashes to pass messages in the dark. It was far too complicated for everyday use, but Louis Braille had worked with it until he'd finally come up with a code of his own.

It was based on a little grid of six dots. With different patterns standing for different letters, it was simple to read. What's more, it meant that blind people could now be taught to write as well. All they needed was a little pointed tool to make the dots with (making sure that they didn't stick it in themselves!).

Over 150 years later, the Braille system (named after Louis) is still the single most important method blind people use for reading and writing. You can get every-thing from Braille calendars to Braille playing cards. While I've been typing this essay, I've been checking every line on the device I mentioned earlier, the one at the bottom of my keyboard. It's called a Braille reader. It converts the letters I've just typed into their Braille codes. Not just for English speakers, either. Louis's system has been used with almost every known language, from Albanian to Zulu.

That is why I nominate Louis Braille. He changed the world for blind people.

Jodi sat back with a sigh of relief. Work done. Time for some music! She'd just dived onto her bed for the CD play-er's remote handset when she heard a knock at her door.

"Jodi?"

"If you're checking up on that essay, Mum, I've just finished it."

Jodi heard the door close, the soft squeak of the chair as her mum sat down at the computer, then nothing more until her essay had been read and Mrs. Webb said, "Very good! I like the bit about the Braille tool. I'd never thought of it as being a dangerous weapon before!"

"Really?"

"Well—maybe once or twice." Jodi's mum hesitantly changed the topic of conversation. "Talking of accidents, how's your leg?"

"No problem, Mum. I told Dad that after it happened."

"No bruises?"

"None that I've spotted."

Jodi said it in such a deadpan way that even her mum missed the joke for a moment. But there was a half smile in her voice as she said, "I hear Luke did well—until the end, I mean."

"Dad said that?"

Jodi picked up the slight pause, the change of tone. "No-o. It was Mr. Blanchflower. He rang to say that he could give us all a lift to the ACB social on Sunday. While he was at it he said that when you both overtook him and Tom, you looked like you'd been running partners for years."

"Wow! What did Dad say about that?"

"Not much," said Mrs. Webb ruefully.

"FEET DOWN, LUKE!" SNAPPED MR. HARMER.

Luke, chair tilted back and heels perched on the edge of

the table, flicked his eyes open. His teacher could be pushed a bit further yet, he reckoned.

"I'm comfy."

"Feet—*DOWN!*"

Misjudgment. The telltale vein on Harmer's neck was already bulging. He was in one of his determined moods. Luke obeyed, but made sure that his chair landed with a crack.

"Thank you," said Mr. Harmer.

The teacher opened his folder and began to take attendance. With a yawn, Luke folded his arms on the table and rested his head on them as if they were a pillow. Apart from a grunt when his name was called, he didn't move until break. That was always fine by Mr. Harmer.

Outside, Luke drifted on an aimless circuit of the school's perimeter fence.

A stray tennis ball rolled to a halt in front of him. He trod on it, keeping his foot there until a swaggering younger boy came for it. He stopped, looking up at Luke.

"Hey. You're Luke Reid, ain't yer?"

"So?"

"Saw yer getting into Viv Defoe's car the other day. Got service again, did yer?"

"Maybe."

The boy's lip curled. "Couldn't have done much, then. Everyone knows Lee Young got Markham for his last job."

"Yeah. He told me," embroidered Luke.

It had been the way in which the boy had breathed Lee

Young's name. Awe. Respect. Luke wanted some of that for a change.

"You know him? Lee Young?" the boy said.

Luke nodded. "And Mig Russell."

"Cool."

Luke picked up the tennis ball and lobbed it back. The boy raced back to his game, looking at Luke over his shoulder as he ran.

Awe. Respect. It felt good.

10

JODI'S "RAVE" WOULDN'T HAVE BEEN RECOGNIZED AS such by the headbangers of Luke's acquaintance. There was no strobe lighting, no pounding music—and far too many adults.

There were adults meeting new arrivals, adults rattling cups and plates, adults laying out tables with board games and playing cards, and adults lugging boxes from one place to another. Only when Luke noticed a guide dog under one of the tables did he realize that not all of the adults were do-gooding helpers. Plenty were in the same position as Jodi. Yet again her words rang in his ears. *It's about me being as normal as I can be.*

"Reid. As you're here, you might as well do something. Go and give Mr. Blanchflower a hand."

Mr. Webb. If he'd been the only adult present, thought Luke, he'd have been one adult too many.

Along with his surly tone, Jodi's father was unhelpfully pointing into space—or to the next best thing, the large panoramic window that formed the whole of one wall of the function room they were in. Luke moved closer to it, hoping for a clue.

He found himself looking down onto a large sports hall. The part immediately beneath the window, the size of a tennis court, had been sectioned off. Gray-haired Mr. Blanchflower had just pushed through the swing doors, loaded down with a large plastic crate of . . . well, Luke couldn't guess what. He wasn't that interested in finding out, either, but if the job was going to take him well clear of Mr. Webb for a while, then he was prepared to make the effort.

"HI. LUKE, ISN'T IT?"

"Yeah." Luke nodded. At least the old boy had used his name.

"What do you know about goalball?" Mr. Blanchflower asked.

Goalball? Luke frowned. Bog all, he thought. "Nothing," he said.

"No reason why you should." Mr. Blanchflower smiled. "But, believe me, it's a popular sport. International teams, the lot."

"So how d'you play it, then?"

"Well, it's a bit like ten-pin bowling and football mixed up together. But me, I don't play it."

"Not young enough, eh?" joked Luke.

"No," said Mr. Blanchflower. "Not blind enough. Here, grab this."

Numbly, his feelings a jumble of embarrassment and confusion, Luke took the end of the bulky reel of thick white tape Mr. Blanchflower had just fished from a plastic crate at his feet. From then on, he simply followed instructions.

"There you go," Mr. Blanchflower said, half an hour later. "One goalball court."

Luke surveyed their handiwork. The tape, he'd quickly discovered, was sticky on one side and rough on the other. They'd used it to mark out a rectangle the size of a tennis court. A few meters from each end, further strips of tape ran from one side of the rectangle to the other. "Kind of penalty areas," Mr. Blanchflower had said. "'Both teams' players have to stay inside their own area."

Luke was able to work out how they managed that from just the little time he'd spent with Jodi. "That's why the tape's rough, yeah? So they can feel it."

"That's right. Goalball players spend most of their time on their hands and knees."

Other things still puzzled Luke, though. "What about the other bits?" he asked. At identical intervals across the "penalty area," Mr. Blanchflower had used smaller sections of tape to make what looked like the calibration marks on a ruler.

"They help the players to work out where they are." He chuckled. "They're not always enough, mind. The referee often has to stop play because somebody's pointing the wrong way! So, Luke, can you guess how the game's played?"

Luke thought for a moment. A cross between ten-pin bowling and football . . . "With a ball?" he said, feeling stupid and stunned at the same time.

"Yep!" Mr. Blanchflower dived into the plastic crate and pulled out what looked like a football with holes in it. "Here you go—catch!"

The ball jangled as it flew through the air and landed in Luke's hands.

"It's a three-a-side game," Mr. Blanchflower went on.

"The players string themselves out across their area. They try to score by bowling the ball into the other team's goal, then defend their own goal when the ball comes shooting back again! Simple, eh?"

Simple? Stopping a whizzing ball you can hear but can't see? It sounded anything but simple.

Animated voices from outside told Luke that the players were arriving. He assumed Jodi would be among them and found himself quite looking forward to seeing how she got on. There was just one further thing puzzling him.

"So where are the goals?" he asked.

"Well spotted, Luke!" Mr. Blanchflower laughed. "We haven't got any. Goalball goals are like three five-a-side goals joined together—they stretch right across the width of each end of the court. Proper goals, with nets and all the gizmos like padded posts, cost a fortune. We haven't been able to afford them. Hopefully, the London Marathon's going to change all that."

"How come?"

"Jodi's sponsorship money. She wants some of it to be used to buy some goals."

"Another thing you almost screwed up," Luke was waiting to hear Mr. Blanchflower add. He didn't, causing Luke to wonder whether he didn't know—or was choosing not to mention it. Either way, he found himself feeling unusually grateful.

"So," Mr. Blanchflower was saying, "until then, we'll do what we've always done: use plastic cones and leave the final decision to the referee—me!"

"And as Mr. Blanchflower can see and we can't, we're in no position to give him any lip!"

It was Jodi. Guided by Mrs. Webb to the hall door, but no farther, she'd been one of a group of players who'd come straight across to where Luke and Mr. Blanchflower were.

"Hi!" Luke grinned. "All right?"

"Good, thanks." Jodi smiled. She turned to Mr. Blanchflower. "We've got a bit of a problem. Sean hasn't turned up, so there're only five of us."

"I told her it doesn't matter 'cos I play like two men!" shouted a hefty lad about Luke's age as he lifted a pair of solid-looking knee pads from Mr. Blanchflower's crate and began to put them on.

Beside him, three others were doing the same. Two were girls, one older and one younger than Jodi. The other Luke recognized as Tom, Mr. Blanchflower's grandson. Each of them sorted themselves out with pads while a scattering of parents and helpers hovered in the background.

Jodi and the big lad obviously had a healthy disrespect for each other. "And I told Rick that just because he's the size of two men doesn't mean he plays like them. Anyway, I don't want him using that as an excuse when his team gets smashed. I've got a better idea."

"Which is?" said Mr. Blanchflower.

"It can be Rick, Beth, and Susila on one side . . ." began Jodi.

"Against you and Tom?" yelled Rick. "You'll get annihilated!"

"No," said Jodi. "Against me, Tom—and Luke."

104

"Me?" cried Luke. "Jodi, ain't you forgetting something?"

"Duh!" Jodi giggled. "You can see, can't you?" She switched quickly to a sharper, but still jokey tone. "Well, we can soon do something about *that*! A full set of equipment for Luke, please, Mr. Blanchflower. Knee pads, elbow pads—and mask!"

Enjoying the fun himself, Mr. Blanchflower was already delving into the depths of his plastic crate.

Luke was beginning to panic. "Jodi—no . . ."

She seemed to sense how he was feeling. "Hey, don't worry. I'm not picking on you. We often pull in sighted helpers to play."

"But—I'll be the only one with a mask on." I don't want to look different. Not here. I don't want to stand out.

"No, you won't," said Jodi. "We all wear them." Even as she spoke, Tom pulled what looked like a large visor over his head.

"Why? I mean . . ."

"Hey, not everyone here's the same as me. Some—Rick, for instance—can see a bit. Just close-up things, and even then they look all blurry. Beth can see farther away, but she says it's like looking through a straw! Anyway, that's why we all wear masks. It evens things up. And it's in the official rules." Jodi added, as if that was an argument that settled matters.

And, as Luke was unable to come up with another excuse, it did. After quickly fitting him out with pads and mask, Mr. Blanchflower guided Luke out onto the playing area.

"Kneel down," said Mr. Blanchflower when they stopped. "Feel the tape marks? Try to stick close to them."

"You're on the right-hand side," Jodi called. "I'm in the center and Tom's on the left. Hey—and it's supposed to be fun, remember!"

Fun? It felt like torture. All Luke could do was try to use the one advantage he had, attempt to retain a picture of the scene in his mind's eye. . . .

Three of them at that end. One of them's got the ball. Old man Blanchflower's blown his whistle. Rattling! The ball's coming our way—fast. Not toward me, though. Diving sounds and a squeal of laughter, both to my left.

"Got it!"

Tom. Sound of him standing up. Grunt of effort. Rattling, going away from us this time—and a cheer from the watching helpers.

"Goal to Jodi's team!" announced Mr. Blanchflower.

Quiet. Ball being returned to a player on the other team, presumably. Rattling coming our way again. Coming my way! But how close? To my left. Not much, though. Move! Almost on me. Put a hand out. It's gone past! Now another squeal. Jodi this time, to my left and back a meter or so, diving and squealing in frustration at the same time. . . .

"Goal to Rick's team!"

"I hate him!" Jodi laughed for Luke's benefit. "He spins them. They go from your right to your left. Did I mention that?"

"No, you didn't!" In spite of himself, Luke was laughing.

Somebody at my side, now. A helper. Ball being put into

106

my hands. Now what? Stand up. Bowl it. Go! Rattling dying away. Thud of ball being stopped at the other end. No whistle or announcement from Mr. B, so no goal. Rattling. The ball's coming straight back again! Where am I? Back to knees, feel for the tape. Can't find it! Ah—got it. No check mark. I'm not in position! Ball coming to my left . . .

"Yeah!"

Jodi's shout of triumph as she saved the shot coincided with Luke's fingers finding his calibration mark. Which of the two gave him the greatest feeling of elation he couldn't have said. But something had, and he yelled "Yeah!" as well. . . .

The game was fast, furious, and—there was no other word for it—fun. Luke hadn't the faintest idea how long they'd been playing or of the score. Neither mattered. The infectious laughter of the others and the sheer craziness of the game had made it an experience he wouldn't forget. So he'd let more than his share of balls go past, but who wouldn't with a kid like Rick at the other end making the ball swerve all over the place?

Getting the hang of him, though. Starts to my right, finishes to my left. He's got it again. Recognize the way he puffs when he stands up. Rattle. Whoosh. Fast rattle, getting closer. It's coming my way! Well to my right, this time. Don't have to move, though, it'll spin back to me. . . . It's not turning! It's sounded different all the other times, changed as it swung. Crafty devil! He's let go a straight one! Dive right! Arms out! Got it!

It was the cleanest catch Luke had made in the whole game. Thudding into his palms, the ball stuck fast as his dive sent Luke rolling over sideways. He was on his feet in a flash, the euphoria of the moment filling his heart and swamping the shouts of those watching.

Quick return! Go for it! Arm back—let 'em have it. Fierce rattle. It's on its way! So why's it stopped? Why the whistle?

"Foul throw, Luke!" Mr. Blanchflower's voice, trying to sound official.

"What? Why?"

Luke heard Jodi now, sounding as if she was in hysterics. "Because you're pointing the wrong way. You must be. I felt the ball whistle past my leg! You've just chucked it into our goal!"

Luke ripped off his mask. Jodi was right. In his excitement he'd lost his bearings. A laughing helper was holding the ball he'd bowled with such hopes of scoring. He felt the blood rushing to his face.

Mr. Blanchflower gave a long blast on his whistle. "Good time to finish. Well played, everybody!"

Jodi immediately found her way to Luke's side. "Own goals don't count, y'know. That's in the rules as well. We've all done it. Last month I nearly knocked Tom's head off!"

Luke felt better at once. "Good thing I didn't hit you, then," he said.

"Yeah! Busting my leg as well as my dad's would have looked really bad!" She was still giggling fit to burst, and Luke was smiling now, too.

Must be infectious, he thought. For, standing at the panoramic window, having been watching the game, Mrs. Webb was also smiling. Mr. Webb was beside her, seated on a chair, his crutches leaning against the glass. He was not smiling.

Surprise, surprise.

"I CAN FINISH OFF HERE, LUKE," SAID MR. BLANCHFLOWER. "Could you guide Tom upstairs for me?"

"Sure." Luke nodded. Jodi had already gone off to get changed, arm in arm with Beth and Susila. Tom obviously lived in his shorts and West Ham football shirt. Waiting for the youngster to grab his elbow, Luke led him out through the sports-hall door and then carefully up the shallow flight of stairs leading to the reception room. Tom chattered all the way.

"That was a great game! Did you cheat?"

"No." Luke smiled.

"I would have. I'd have peeped under my mask! Why didn't you?"

"Because your grandad would have seen me, for starters."

"He would an' all! He'd have sent you off!"

"Yeah." Luke laughed. "Given me a red card!"

They'd reached the top of the stairs. Tom, a step behind so that he could tell when Luke had stopped climbing, joined him on the level.

"Yeah!" he echoed brightly, only to become thoughtful in an instant. "What does a red card look like, Luke?"

"A red card? Well, it's square-shaped. And . . ." *Red*.

What else could he say? Red is red. How do you describe a color? Then the memory of Jodi's bright flowers gave him the answer.

"And hot," he said. "Red's a hot color. For refs to wave at hotheaded players!"

He led Tom into the reception room. The youngster turned his face up toward Luke.

"You're cool."

He'd said it in a way that reminded Luke of the kid in the playground. With a touch of awe. With respect. But this felt better, by a mile.

"No, he's not."

It was a scowling Mr. Webb. Having left his spot by the window, he was now perched on a chair just inside the door.

"He's not cool at all, Tom. He's a thief."

11

VIV DEFOE'S LITTLE OFFICE WAS CRAMPED AND CLUTTERED. Box files sat on sagging shelves. Two ancient filing cabinets bulged with yet more papers, the drawers too full to close properly. The probation officer's small desk seemed to have been designed to fit into the little space that was left. Sitting uncomfortably on the equally undersized chair, Viv reminded Luke of a big boy who'd been sent to the infants' class as a punishment.

Another day, Luke might have said so. Not today. He wasn't in the mood for happy talk. He came straight to the point.

"I don't want to do it anymore, Viv."

Viv smiled. "What, thieving? I'm delighted to hear it, Luke."

"You know what I mean. Working with that lot. The guide running. I wanna do something else."

"Why?"

"You know why. Him."

"Mr. Webb?"

Luke nodded. "He hates me."

Viv stood up, stretching his back as if he'd been in a cramped position for too long. "Can you blame him?"

The question caught Luke by surprise. Could he blame

Mr. Webb for hating him? He'd really never thought about it. Viv filled the silence with some more ammunition.

"If it wasn't for you he wouldn't have broken his leg. If it wasn't for you he'd still be able to help his daughter. If it wasn't for you he might still have his car. . . ."

"I didn't take it!"

"But you haven't helped catch those who did, have you?"

Luke wheeled out his, by now, well-oiled lie. "I don't know who took it," he recited, before switching the subject back to what he wanted to talk about. "And I don't want to carry on with this blind lot for my service. Get me something else to do."

"Why? Why pack it in before you've given it a chance?"

"I *have* given it a chance!"

"Two sessions? Oh, well done, Luke. Very good. Full marks for stamina."

Viv was angry now, angrier than Luke had ever seen him before. He jabbed a finger at the rows of boxes, opened a bulging filing-cabinet drawer, and slammed it shut again.

"Look at this lot. East Med kids, West Med kids. And plenty of Town kids in case you think you're always the ones being picked on. Every one given a chance to sort themselves out. Some"—he glared at Luke—"two chances, three chances, more. You may not like the system, Luke, but it's giving you a damn sight more of a chance than you're giving it."

He sat down again, still angry, leaning forward on his tiny chair to make his point. "How many sessions do you think Jodi's given it? Did she give up after the first two? Of course she didn't. But then you're not thinking about her, are you? You're just thinking about yourself."

"You're sounding like old man Webb!" snapped Luke.

"Maybe because he's right!" shouted Viv. He leaned back, calming himself but not softening his line. "So you had an accident on the track and he gave you an earful. Jodi wasn't hurt. She doesn't hold it against you, does she?"

"And the rest." Luke glowered, finally spilling what had gnawed at him throughout the rest of the evening at the Broke, what Luke had been unable to tell Viv as the probation officer had driven him home. "He told one of the younger kids I was a thief."

"You are, Luke."

Viv said it quietly, but the probation officer's words couldn't have echoed in Luke's head louder if he'd bawled them through a megaphone. Luke didn't—couldn't—respond. Viv seemed to sense it and broke the silence himself.

"Why give up now?" he asked. "Because you know what's going to happen if you do, don't you? I can find you a bit of graffiti cleaning easy, but at the end of it you'll be off to Markham. Is that what you want?"

Luke shrugged. That wasn't what he wanted. He desperately didn't want that. But he didn't want to put up with Mr. Webb anymore, either. When it came down to it, right down to rock bottom, he didn't know what he wanted.

Standing up abruptly, Viv pulled his jacket from the back of his chair and thrust it on. "OK, then. Let's go."

"Go? Where?"

"To the Webbs' place. I'm not telling them. You can do it

yourself. Tell Jodi to her face you're going to let her down."

"She won't care," said Luke, though he didn't believe that.

Viv was playing it hard. "Then it'll be easy for you, won't it?" he said.

He'd opened his office door and was waiting. Luke didn't move, just stared sullenly down at his hands. He couldn't do it. To Mr. Webb, easy. Given the chance, he'd let rip at him and love it—but not to her. Not to the only person who'd ever said she trusted him.

Viv quietly sat down again, so quietly that Luke couldn't help wondering if he'd been the victim of some brilliant acting.

"Hey. At least give it another session. The next one's Saturday morning, isn't it?"

Luke nodded. He looked at Viv. "Can you stay this time? Keep old man Webb off my back?"

"You won't have to worry about Mr. Webb this Saturday. When we had our meeting, he told me he wouldn't be there. Physiotherapy session or something like that."

Luke brightened slightly. "No misery guts? Be a pity to miss that, eh?"

Viv stood up and opened the door for Luke, this time with a smile. "I'll be round to pick you up, then."

Luke paused at the door. "How about giving me a lift to the Riverside afterward?"

"No can do. I've got other things on. What do you need at the Riverside?"

"Got to get my dad a card. It's his birthday on Saturday. He'll only get it a day late this year."

Luke didn't bother explaining why the card would be late. He figured Viv had already worked out that Sunday was the day Luke's mum found easiest for prison visiting.

THE SATURDAY-MORNING TRAINING SESSION WENT BETTER than Luke could have hoped.

Viv had driven off the moment Jodi arrived. The parent who had given Jodi a lift to the Broke turned out to be puffing, gray-haired Mr. Blanchflower again—with his grandson, Tom. Luke drifted slowly across the parking lot as Tom and Jodi climbed out of Mr. Blanchflower's ancient but beautifully maintained estate car.

"Hi," Luke said uncertainly.

Tom gave him a flicker of a smile, full of doubt. But Jodi was clearly in high spirits as usual. "Hiya, Luke! Feeling fit?"

Luke shrugged, then cursed himself for being stupid. "Not bad," he said. "How about you?"

"Great." Jodi's hand was already feeling for his elbow. "All ready to dive into action!"

HER GOOD MOOD HAD CARRIED OVER ONTO THE RUNNING track. After the warm-ups they'd done a steady lap. It had gone well. Luke had kept to his position, told Jodi when to turn and straighten, and definitely made sure her feet didn't land anywhere near the edge of the track.

"Great!" she said as Luke brought them to a halt. "That felt really easy."

"Yeah?"

"Yeah. I wasn't worried at all. You should have been able to tell that from the way I was running."

Luke frowned. "How?"

"My knees weren't knocking together!" hooted Jodi.

Still laughing, she felt for the watch on her wrist. Luke had seen it before, but only then did it occur to him to wonder how she could tell the time. The question was quickly answered. A quick press of a button on the side and the glass face sprang open for Jodi to run her fingers over the raised hands.

"Smart watch," he said, impressed.

"Birthday present," said Jodi, adding, "from my parents." She gave a sad little sigh. "Oh, I do appreciate them really, y'know. They've always done their best for me. It can't have been easy having their baby daughter go blind on them."

Luke hesitated. "How . . ."

"How did it happen? Just a bum deal when my genes were sorted out. There's blindness on my mum's side, apparently. A hereditary disease called *retinitis pigmentosa*. Just my luck for it to jump a generation and land on me. Still, it could have been worse. Sufferers usually lose their sight when they're in their forties or fifties."

"That would have been *worse*?"

"Of course it would. You don't miss what you've never really had." She waggled her wrist brightly. "And I wouldn't have gotten to own a really cool watch! It's a stopwatch as well, y'know. Want to test it?"

"To do what?"

"See how long it takes us to run a mile."

"A mile!"

"The mini-marathon is over two and a half miles. You need to start building up to guide me for the full distance. . . ."

Luke hadn't been able to argue against that. Besides, without Mr. Webb glowering at him from his bench, he was feeling good himself.

They'd started steadily, though, nothing heroic. Round the first lap and into the second, round that and into the third. Apart from the odd times when he got out of step or didn't warn Jodi about bends at exactly the right time for her to start the turn, they'd gone well.

It was as they moved into the fourth and final lap that he began to feel it. That first session they'd run individual laps, with a nice break in between. Now his chest was hurting and his legs were feeling as though they had lead weights attached to them.

"You want to stop?"

Jodi. She wouldn't have failed to notice that he was gasping rather than breathing.

"No way. I'm fine."

"Sure?"

"Sure." Luke gritted his teeth, even as he grunted a warning that the final bend was on them. "Slow left—now!"

But he was struggling. As they came out of the bend, the strap linking them was flapping loosely. Jodi was actually going faster than he was. If he couldn't pick up speed, he'd be holding her back—

"Stop!" cried Jodi.

Even as he slowed to a mightily relieved halt, Luke was

looking at Jodi in surprise. She'd been going so well. Now she was clutching her side.

"Sorry," she said. "Terrible stitch. I had to stop."

Luke felt like cheering. But two things stopped him: a complete lack of breath—and a sudden screech of pain coming from over by the long-jump pit.

"That's Tom!" cried Jodi at once. "What's happened?"

Luke looked across. Mr. Blanchflower was already kneeling in the sand beside his writhing grandson.

"Sprained his ankle, looks like," said Luke. "Maybe worse."

"Lead me over there, Luke. He's broken it before now. He may need to go to the hospital for an X ray."

Luke felt her grip his elbow, almost pushing him forward. "You're telling me he does the long jump, too? Why?"

"Because he can," said Jodi simply.

Luke led Jodi across. Mr. Blanchflower saw her coming and drew her over so that she could help him calm the still-yelling Tom.

Only then, as he watched her talking without the slightest sign of difficulty, did Luke realize that she'd never had a stitch at all. She'd known he was in trouble. That's why she'd called a halt—to save him from letting her down again.

What had Mrs. Mousse, the magistrate, said about them? *A quite remarkable family?* He wasn't so sure about Mr. and Mrs. Webb—there was nothing remarkable about them treating him like a turd, plenty of people did that—but when it came to Jodi, he was starting to see what she meant.

And it was only the start. The next installment came

almost at once. While a couple of other helpers were shaking their heads as they studied Tom's ankle, Mr. Blanchflower led Jodi back across to Luke. "Now you're sure about this, Jodi?" he was saying.

Jodi took hold of Luke's elbow again. "Positive. I've got my mobile with me. I can call one and Dad will pay when I get home."

Looking grateful and concerned at the same time, Mr. Blanchflower went back to his grandson.

"What's going on?" Luke asked.

"Mr. Blanchflower's taking Tom to the hospital. I told him not to worry about having to give me a lift home. He thinks I'm calling a taxi."

"How do you mean, *he thinks?*"

"Because I'm not. It's only a couple of miles. You can guide me."

"Me?"

"Yes, you. Hey, I'll do a deal with you. We don't have to run, we can walk it! Yeah?"

Luke shook his head. There was no point arguing with Jodi, even if he'd wanted to—which he didn't. "Yeah." He grinned. "I'd better borrow that phone and tell Viv I don't need a lift after all."

LUKE SOON DISCOVERED THAT GUIDING JODI AROUND A running track was simple compared to a busy street. But, while he was feeling a mixture of quiet pride at being able to do it and silent terror in case he failed, Jodi seemed to be loving every minute of it.

"This is more like it!" She laughed as Luke only just managed to avoid guiding her into a lamppost. "The London Marathon's going to be just like this, Luke. Obstacles everywhere! I'm trusting you to save me."

"Your dad wouldn't trust me as far as he could throw me."

"That's him, not me." Jodi gave another peal of happy laughter. "Besides, I'm a runner not a shot-putter!"

They'd arrived at a road junction controlled by a set of lights. Normally Luke would have dived across, threading his way between the cars and giving lip to any who dared to honk at him. Not today.

"Stop," he said, halting at the curb.

"Link Road," said Jodi. She didn't wait for Luke to ask how she knew. "Dad's always moaning about these lights. Says they wait too long for walkers to cross."

On the other side of the road the little green man started to flash. Simultaneously, the high-pitched beep began the racket that Luke had always found so irritating. As Jodi nudged him and said, "Chop-chop, time to move. You deaf or something?" he knew it would never annoy him again.

They walked on, heading for West Med's version of the Bridge. As with the East Med estate, West Med was linked to the Town by a narrow metallic footbridge spanning the expressway. The only difference, Luke noticed as they reached it, was that West Med's bridge was rustier.

Across they went. Luke was now slowing down much less often. Jodi's confidence in him was showing. If he gave her an instruction, or even if he just smoothly changed direction to avoid somebody coming the other way, she followed him at once. By the time they'd reached the shabby clutch of shops at the northern end of Rigby Road, he felt confident enough to take a chance.

"There's a One-Stop shop I want to go into," he said. "We're just coming up to it."

"I know."

Luke couldn't help it this time. "How d'you know? Go on, tell me."

"We turned left at the traffic lights. That's how I knew we were heading for the footbridge. And I'd have known we'd reached it even if I couldn't hear the traffic on the expressway. It's made of metal, so it sounds and feels different when you walk on it. Then there's the chip shop at the corner, I could smell that before we got anywhere near it! Same goes for the café we've just passed, especially when they've got bacon sandwiches on the go. And as I know the One-Stop is three shops down from that . . . bingo!"

"Admit it," said Luke. "You don't need me, do you?"

Jodi pushed his arm gently. "Yes, I do. Come on, there's something I want to get from the One-Stop as well."

Inside the shop, Jodi was received like an old friend. An assistant hurried over and took her off Luke's arm. Leaving them, he strolled casually round to scan the racks of cards.

Happy Birthday to the World's Best Dad!
Happy Birthday to a Great Dad!
HAVE A GREAT BIRTHDAY, DAD. YOU DESERVE IT.

Luke settled for one with plain *Happy Birthday, Dad*. It was a decent size. Not too small, but not so large that he couldn't easily slip it out of sight inside his jacket. He glanced up at the convex security mirror in the corner. The assistant had finished looking after Jodi. Now she was standing at her counter—looking at him. He was going to have to pay.

"What did you buy?" asked Jodi outside.

"Birthday card. For my dad." Luke changed the subject fast. "How about you?"

Jodi dipped into the paper bag she was holding. "Flower seeds. Stocks. They smell beautiful when they come up." She felt for Luke's hand and put one of the two packets she'd bought between his fingers. "For you."

"Me!" Luke didn't mean to scoff, but he couldn't help it. "Seeds? Where d'you think I'm going to stick these? I live ten floors up, no garden, no nothing. You keep 'em."

"You don't need a garden. Put some earth in a wooden box. Anything. Plant them and see what happens."

A shout from the café doorway, three doors away, stopped him from arguing any further.

"Hey, Lukey! Who's the babe?"

It was Mig Russell, mouth full and a half-eaten bacon sandwich in his hand. At the table just inside the door, Lee Young was sipping from a can. He joined in with a call of "Nice one!"

Russell gave an openmouthed laugh, spraying bread crumbs into the air. "We'll be seeing yer, Lukey. You'd better believe it."

They hadn't recognized Jodi as the girl from the parking

lot, realized Luke. No surprise. It had been so quick. Plus, he told himself yet again, the only reason they got so close to her in the stolen 4x4 was that they didn't spot her until the last moment.

Even so, Luke spun away quickly—so quickly that he even forgot to hand back the packets of seeds before leading Jodi on down Rigby Road.

"Who was that?" she asked quietly.

"Nobody. A couple of lads I know. Dunno what they're doing over this side. They live in East Med."

Another question, still posed quietly. "Got names, have they?"

"Lee Young, Mig Russell," he answered without thinking.

They were at Jodi's home. As Luke unlatched the front gate, a movement from behind the lace curtains told him that Mrs. Webb was on her way to open the door. "See you next training session, then," he said.

Jodi nodded, but she'd lost her sparkle. She turned to face him, forcing him to face her. "You said you didn't know who took our car."

Luke caught his breath. "What?"

"But you do, don't you? And so do I, now. Their names are Lee Young and Mig Russell. I told you I'd recognize their voices if I heard them again."

Luke swallowed hard. There was no ducking it, now. He had to tell her, make her see sense.

"Jodi, they're not my friends. I knew *about* them, that's all—and what they'd do to me if I told on them. If I was to breathe a word, I'd be done."

Mrs. Webb was on the doorstep now. She hadn't rushed forward to help Jodi, but Luke was too preoccupied to appreciate the compliment.

"Jodi, please!" he hissed. "Promise me you won't say anything!"

"Oh, Luke," she murmured softly. "Who'd believe a blind girl?"

12

THERE WAS A LINE, AS ALWAYS. MOSTLY WOMEN AND children, it stretched for twenty meters down the road in full view of the passing traffic. Drivers and passengers would look out, point, shake their heads. Luke could guess what they were saying. . . .

Visiting time. Waiting for the gates to open. Poor devils. Must be horrible having one of your own locked up. Still, probably serves them right.

Up ahead, the gate officer must have done his stuff. The line was beginning to shuffle forward. Luke moved with them, hands in his pockets, trying to think of something he could say to the man inside.

Visiting time wasn't limited as much as it used to be. Once it had just been twice a month, but now they could have come most days if they'd wanted to—and if Luke's mum had been able to afford it. She couldn't. Underground-train fares across London made it an expensive outing. And it wasn't as if it was a fun trip, like going to the seaside or the zoo. Once his brother and sister had been told—again—who the strange man was, they invariably spent the rest of the time jumping on and off their chairs and generally making a racket. His mum had only gotten them here quietly today by telling them that it was Daddy's birthday. Luke didn't like to think about the stink they were going to kick up when they discovered that birthdays in Her Majesty's prison, Wormwood Scrubs, weren't celebrated with cake and ice cream.

Through the gate and into the entrance area, all chattering—even of the frequent visitors—stilled by the sound of the gate officer locking them in.

Then they were clicking through a new turnstile arrangement as if they were going into a football stadium to watch a big game. A short walk, then up a flight of stairs, and they were being ushered into the visitors' hall.

His dad was there already, in his usual spot over on the far side. Until not so long ago they'd had to sit with all the other visitors on one side of a series of tables joined together as if they were at a street party—except that guests at street parties didn't whisper so that they couldn't be overheard by their neighbors. The place had been fixed up since then. Now they sat on soft seats, grouped round low coffee tables.

One thing hadn't changed, though. Circling the walls, their eyes never still, stood the prison guards. Luke found that he couldn't ignore them, however hard he tried.

His dad didn't look up until they reached him, as if they'd disturbed him mid-thought. He forced a smile. "Hi. All right, then?"

It was a general welcome, though, looking at none of them in particular. Luke's mum, Billy and Jade hanging on to her skirt, leaned forward and kissed him. Luke hovered until the others had finished, then simply said "Hi" and sat down. Conversation began awkwardly, like strangers meeting in a railway car.

Mum: "How are you?"

Dad: "All right, I suppose. You?"

A nod and a shrug. "Fine. Billy had a bit of a cold. He's all right now, though."

Jade: "And I fell over and hurt my knee!" Pointing at the grubby square of sticking tape.

Billy, still holding a grudge: "She broke my best car."

Jade: "Your car hurt my knee!"

They were off then, dominating the conversation, gathering all the attention. Luke felt not much more than human wallpaper as he sat studying his father.

He'd gotten older-looking. His fingers seemed more stained from the cigarettes he smoked. His skin was grayer, the once vivid-blue tattoo on his forearm now looked pale and washed-out.

Would that happen to him if he ended up in Markham? Would he come out looking all gray and lifeless? Luke dismissed the thought at once. Lee Young and Mig Russell had come through it all right, hadn't they?

But then there was a bit of a difference between four months and the time his dad had spent locked up. Two years for a spate of shop burglaries. Four years for aggravated burglary and possessing a firearm. Out for a while, then back in for another two years just before Billy was born. Out again, for long enough to get involved with a fraud that lost half a dozen old people their life savings. A four-year stretch, this time. Jade had been born on the day he was sentenced. How many years did that make?

Luke's calculations were interrupted by the sound of his

mum's voice, taking advantage of a brief lull in Billy and Jade's chatter to trill a trying-to-be-cheerful note, "Anyway—happy birthday!"

Billy handed over his homemade card—a huge thing created at the local play group and splattered with enough poster paint to have decorated a small room. It dwarfed Jade's scrawled stick man on scrap paper, and the sight made her scowl. She perked up when the presents came out, the bar of chocolate she was given to hand to the strange man being satisfyingly larger than Billy's pack of cigarettes. Over by the wall, one of the prison guards noted the exchange. It would be his duty to examine those birthday packages the moment visiting was over. He didn't like doing it, but rules were rules.

"Luke?"

Mum was looking at him. So was his dad, in a half-interested kind of way. Luke pulled out the card he'd bought the day before. "Yeah. Happy birthday," he said.

His dad took it, ripped open the envelope with his thumb, glanced at the card inside, now bearing a scribbled message. He grunted something, which might have been "Thanks" but then again might not.

Mum was still looking Luke's way. "That all?" she asked.

Luke didn't realize what she was on about, at least not until Billy chirped up. "Luke hasn't brought a present! *I* brought a present."

"And *I* did!" squawked Jade, not to be outdone in their never-ending battle for supremacy.

At first, Luke felt ashamed. At the One-Stop shop the day

before, he hadn't had enough money to buy both a card and a present. He'd intended to go out and get something later, but for one reason or another, it had slipped his mind. Mixed in with his shame, though, was a silent fury: Why should he have bought him a present? Taken the risk of stealing something for him, even? Did people usually give presents to strangers?

Why he did what he did next, Luke couldn't explain. Maybe it was the anger he felt at being put on the spot. Maybe it was the shame of not having something to give his own father, no matter what he thought of him. Whatever, when Luke realized there was something else in his pocket— still where he'd stuffed it as he'd hurried Jodi away from the shouts of Lee Young and Mig Russell—he didn't think, just handed it over.

"A packet of seeds?"

It was obvious Luke's dad couldn't believe it. He was smiling, but it wasn't the loving kind of smile he'd given Billy and Jade. This smile was a combination of disgust and . . . Luke didn't know, something he couldn't pin down.

"What am I supposed to do with seeds? Feed 'em to the birds?"

Already Luke was regretting what he'd done, regretting not simply claiming that he hadn't been able to afford anything. They couldn't have argued with that. As it was, all he could think to do now was repeat what Jodi had said to him.

"You don't need a garden. Put some earth in a wooden box. Anything. Plant them and see what happens."

The feeling Luke couldn't identify was still in his dad's

eyes, getting stronger if anything. "What do you think this place is, Luke?" he said, stubbing out his cigarette with short, powerful jabs. "A holiday camp? Eh? A hotel full of happy guests having a fun time? Do you?"

"No . . ."

"Too right, it isn't! There's six hundred men in here—all hard as nails. If you're not as tough as them they'll tear you apart. And you want me to . . . to grow *flowers*!"

Luke's dad began to laugh, a hard, mirthless laugh, as though it were stuck in his throat and he were trying to force it out. He bent forward, his shoulders shaking as he turned the seed packet over and over in his fingers, looking at the picture on the front and the instructions on the back, which said *Plant in April for an abundance of flowers from July to the first frosts*. It was only after thirty seconds or so that Luke realized his dad was no longer laughing.

He was crying.

The feeling Luke had noticed in his dad's eyes, the feeling he hadn't seen before and couldn't pin down—it was pain.

Over by the wall, one of the guards was shifting position— not dramatically, but enough to check what was going on. Quickly, Luke's dad wiped the tears away with his cuff, fumbled a cigarette out of his birthday pack, and lit it. Then he snaked a hand across the table to take that of Luke's mum.

"When I get out," he muttered, "I'm going straight."

"You said that before, Dave," she replied flatly.

"I know. But this time I mean it. Really mean it." He linked his fingers in hers. "You know what hit me when I woke up this morning? I'm thirty-five. Thirty-five years old.

And I've spent ten of them inside. Ten of my birthdays behind bars."

"And ten of mine!" Luke wanted to scream. He was blinking back tears of his own, wishing he could think of something to say that would help, something to make up for the poxy packet of seeds. Nothing came to mind.

Then it was too late. The moment had passed, or so it seemed. His dad shook his head, like a boxer who'd been on the receiving end of a surprise punch, and sat back again. Billy and Jade grabbed their opportunity to fill the silence—and the rest of the visiting hour—with their squabbling and chatter.

But when the time came for them to leave, Luke found his arm being clutched to hold him back while his mum shepherded the two young ones out of the visitors' hall. Only then did his dad ask, "How's it going? The probation?"

Luke nodded. "OK, I suppose."

He felt his arm being gripped tighter, so tight that it hurt. "Stick with it, Luke. You hear? Don't end up like me, wasting your life away in a place like this. Promise me."

Luke turned to face him. His father, the stranger. "It ain't easy."

A hiss. Desperate, almost. "Promise me!"

Another promise? First Jodi, now Dad? He nodded. "Yeah, all right. I promise."

It seemed like he'd heard what he wanted. Pausing only to pick up his cards and presents, Luke's dad turned away to join the silent line of prisoners waiting to return to their cells.

Luke hurried to catch up with his mum, Billy, and Jade. Tears were pricking at his own eyes now. He was suddenly feeling wildly, amazingly, unforgettably happy. For behind him, the coffee table was bare.

No chocolate. No cigarettes. And no packet of seeds.

13

THE GOOD FEELING FROM THE BIRTHDAY VISIT HAD stayed with Luke for over three weeks. What's more, it seemed to have spread beyond thoughts of his dad. Buds of color had begun to appear in other corners of his life.

Jodi, for a start. Telling her about Lee Young and Mig Russell seemed to have been the best thing he could have done. She hadn't mentioned them since.

Then there was his service, in general. He'd begun to feel a little more comfortable with it. He'd helped out at a couple of evening get-togethers of the ACB, just serving refreshments and the like. Being thanked for doing nothing more than delivering a cup of tea and a cookie was strangely nice.

It was on refreshment duty, too, that Mrs. Webb had surprised him. It had happened at an after-school library event. She'd brought Jodi on the bus to a group that met every month at the local library. With Annie, a librarian, in charge, the group members would spend an hour discussing Braille books they'd read or speaking books they'd listened to. Luke had had a nasty moment when Annie had tried to bring him into the conversation, asking what he'd read lately.

"Er . . . not a lot. Not really . . ."

Mrs. Webb had rescued him, suggesting it was time the post-discussion refreshments were prepared. As they collected glasses and plates from the small library staff room, there'd been an awkward silence. Luke had wanted to break it by saying something—anything. But all that came to mind was "Thanks, the last thing I read was a police handout on how youth courts worked." In any event, Mrs. Webb had beaten him to it.

"I want to say thank you," she said quietly.

"What for?"

"Helping Jodi."

I didn't have much choice, did I? Luke added mentally, only to feel immediately ashamed. "No problem." He shrugged.

Mrs. Webb piled some glasses onto a tray. "I suppose she's told you what an old mother hen she thinks I am."

Luke smiled ruefully. "That's what mums are for, innit? Telling you stuff and worrying about you?"

Jodi's mum had smiled herself, then. "True. But sometimes we can, well . . . overdo it."

She'd said no more. Just handed the tray over to Luke, then followed him as he carried it out of the door.

Yes, some things had really changed. . . .

LUKE SLIPPED OUT OF BED. IN HIS OWN CORNER OF THE tiny bedroom, his brother, Billy, thumb in his mouth, didn't stir. The thumb stayed in place while Luke dressed and was still being quietly sucked as he clicked the front door shut and began to move silently along the walkway.

It was six-thirty in the morning, before dawn. In the past week, it had been getting uncomfortably light at this time, but the clocks going forward had restored things. Even so, Luke had put on the darkest gear he had: navy blue sweatshirt, charcoal-colored jeans.

There was no point in drawing attention to himself. For one thing, he wasn't anxious to have Nasty and Weary, or any other squad-car combo, stop him for twenty questions about what he was doing and where he was going.

Mostly, though, he was still a bit embarrassed. He felt like pinching himself to make sure this really was him, Luke Reid, getting up early in the morning to go for a training run.

He'd started the day after the birthday visit to the prison, inspired by his dad's resolve to embark on a new way of life. That and the training-session memory of how Jodi had saved him from collapsing at the last bend by pretending to have a stitch. That had been after they'd run just a mile. In less than a month's time, he was going to have to manage over twice that distance if he was to guide her successfully round the mini-marathon course.

The course . . . that was another problem. They'd be running on London's rough and bumpy roads, not a smooth running track. So he had to get used to running on roads, get used to spotting the kind of dangers he'd have to steer Jodi away from. Mr. Webb had already been going on about them road running together, of course.

"You'll be going outside next week, Reid," he'd warned at their most recent training session. "You may think you're doing OK, but I'm telling you for nothing that road running is a different game. You've got to keep your wits about you 110 percent."

Jodi had put the moaning in perspective. "Hear that?" she'd said as they'd set off for one final lap. "He thinks you're doing OK."

"No, he doesn't. He thinks *I* think I'm doing OK," Luke had countered.

"You dummy! He wouldn't have said *anything* if you weren't!"

Maybe she was right. Either way, what Jodi's father thought of him didn't matter anymore. Luke wanted to do this for himself, for Jodi . . . and, in a funny sort of way, for his own dad. If his dad could change his life and go straight, then so could Luke. He hadn't even thought about going out thieving since the prison visit.

At the bottom of Foxglove House, Luke opened and closed the rusting metal door as silently as possible. Then he checked his watch and began to run.

He went off at a nice steady pace, the sort of pace Jodi preferred until she was in a comfortable rhythm. He ran at the side of the road, not on the pavement. It had a more realistic feel about it and, besides, the East Med roads were in better condition than the cracked and weed-infested pavements.

His route was one he'd worked out from a local map. It took him to the southern tip of the estate, where it met the River Thames. From there all he had to do was hop across an overgrown vacant lot and he was on the barren service road the delivery trucks rumbled along to get to the Riverside Centre. They wouldn't start arriving in force for another hour, so at this time it was good and quiet. What's more, it was just about the right distance—almost three miles there and back.

Would this be the day?

The thought pinged into his mind at once. He tried to push it away, stop the tension it caused. He couldn't.

Would this be the day? The day he broke twenty minutes?

He hadn't managed it yet. He'd improved, for sure. He was quicker than when he started, easily. His and Jodi's time over a mile had improved steadily. It must have—Mr. Webb hadn't moaned about it recently! But they hadn't yet tried the full distance at full pace. As her father had pointed out at every opportunity, Jodi's best time was twenty minutes. That was the time Luke wanted to beat, the time he had to beat, if he wasn't going to hold her back.

Would this be the day he'd do it?

He had reached the vacant lot. A big sign announced that the patch was earmarked for new houses, a few more colored-in patches on the painting-by-numbers—fresh starts for a lucky few.

Luke ran on, concentrating on keeping his footing amid the half bricks and bonfire remains. Then he was out onto the service road and lengthening his stride.

A lone car swept past on the other side of the road, headlights ablaze. The driver glanced over at Luke, shaking his head as if wondering what sort of lunatic dragged himself out of bed to go for a run at this time of the morning.

Luke almost waved. He didn't feel like a lunatic. With the

mild breeze ruffling at his sweatshirt and over his face, he felt alive and free. Even the vile smells wafting across from the Thames seemed sweeter somehow.

On he went, moving smoothly, breathing evenly, ticking off his private landmarks as he passed them: the flickering streetlamp; the dumped fridge on the shoulder; the huge dark splotch on the white concrete where a truck had shed some of its load of paint tins; the builder's Dumpster long since forgotten by whoever put it there.

Soon—surprisingly soon—he'd reached the point at which the service road began to arc toward the outskirts of the Riverside Centre. Halfway—and in just under ten minutes! Trying not to let the thought affect his rhythm, Luke began to head back.

Now the landmarks came at him in reverse. The builder's Dumpster, and he was still moving well. At the paint splotch, he could feel a dull ache creeping into his legs. By the time he'd reached the abandoned fridge, he was still in control, but breathing more heavily.

Then, no more than a hundred meters before the flickering streetlamp, it hit him again—a sudden, overwhelming exhaustion. His whole body felt as though it were crumbling. And now his brain, the one part of him that seemed to have energy to spare, started playing its usual tricks.

Why was he doing this? What was the point? Stop! If he stopped now, the pain would go away. Stop, stop, stop . . .

Every time so far he'd done just that: he'd stopped, bent low, waited for the hurt to ease, felt the seconds tick away with every thump of his pounding heart. But not this time.

This time he resisted, gritting his teeth, trying to blank out the beguiling phantom voice.

He'd reached the flickering streetlamp. The edge of the vacant lot was in sight. Foxglove House wasn't far beyond that. Luke stumbled on, his legs no longer feeling as though they belonged to his body. They were moving of their own accord, like two robotic limbs programmed to find their way home. Now, with every step, his mind was fighting back, too, resisting with a fierce determination that Luke didn't know he possessed.

Don't give up! he told himself. Keep going! Stick with it, like you promised Dad!

The vacant lot nearly finished him. His eyesight blurring with the effort, he didn't see a slab of builder's rubble jutting out of the ground. Tripping over it, he lost his footing, landing on all fours. Somehow, he kept going. Moving forward in a crazy crablike crawl, which skinned both knees, he somehow forced himself upright without actually stopping.

And then he was across it. The cracked paving stones of the pathway leading to Foxglove House felt like silk beneath his feet. His gasping, searing lungs were forgotten. The dark voices were silent. The finish line was in sight.

Luke flogged himself forward, barely aware of what he was doing, knowing only that nothing short of a brick wall could stop him now. Thirty meters, twenty, ten . . . and then he was there, throwing himself at the rust-stained metal door at the base of Foxglove House as if it were a long-lost relative. Through tear-blurred eyes he looked at his watch. Nineteen minutes, fifty-three seconds.

Chest heaving, his legs on fire, Luke turned his back to the door and slid down to the ground. The whole of East Med seemed to be spinning before his eyes. He couldn't focus on anything, not even the graffiti on the wall opposite. *Death to all grass scum.*

He'd done it! And if he'd done it once, he could do it again. He wouldn't let Jodi down.

He really believed that.

14

"FOUR WEEKS IN A ROW, LUKE?" SAID MR. HARMER ACIDLY. "I'll have to think of putting you forward for a good attendance medal."

Luke slid into his seat and waited for the next crack. Harmer never made do with just the one.

"Not to mention most improved student. I mean, four weeks' attendance—if you're not careful you'll be learning something!"

Luke didn't respond. For all his sarcasm, Harmer had a point. Luke's recent attendance had certainly been something of a record. His behavior, too, for that matter. It was strange. His early-morning runs, especially now that he'd cracked the twenty-minute barrier, made him feel good—and sitting in school all day seemed more bearable. He'd even started listening more, thinking it would be nice to have an answer the next time Jodi's library group asked what he'd read lately.

And when boredom did overtake him, Luke had still found he could usefully employ the time to dream about what it was going to be like to guide Jodi along the London Marathon route.

That's what he did throughout the tutorial session, stirring only to heave Terry Fisher's heavy backpack away as his late-arriving desk partner dumped it down on his foot. Twenty minutes later, Luke had to shift the bag again, this time so that he could join the exodus of those from his lower-set group who—unlike that nerd Fisher—were heading for the math block and a double period of torture by calculator. When it ended, he found Mr. Harmer waiting for him outside in the corridor.

"Fisher's cell phone," snapped Harmer. "Where is it?"

Luke, his mind still numb from math, didn't catch on at first. "His what?"

"Cell phone. Against the rules, I know, but Fisher brings his in. Amazingly, he's got himself a girlfriend in another school and the highlight of his day is to sneak off and call her between lessons. This morning he looks in his bag and what do you know? Missing cell phone."

"So? What's that got to do with me?"

"According to Fisher, you were the last person to touch his bag."

"To stop it from breaking my foot!" retorted Luke. "I shoved it out of the way."

"That's all?"

"Yeah!"

Harmer's whole body tightened. As he moved his face closer, the teacher's voice dropped to a hiss that only Luke could hear. "You know what hacks me off about this country, Luke? The way we give people chances they don't deserve. People like you."

"What about me?" Luke himself was angry now.

"You're a thief, that's what. You steal and get caught and

steal again and get caught again, but still nobody's got the sense to make sure you get punished. Really punished. Shut away, where you can't do any harm. Oh, no. You're just allowed to run around, free as a bird."

Luke tried to turn, but Harmer was blocking his way, memories of countless disrupted lessons and acts of insolence fueling his rage. "I drive through East Med every morning. I've seen you running. Well, make the most of it, you little creep, because it's not going to last. One day you'll be done."

The teacher backed away, then spoke at a normal volume so that everybody filing along the corridor could hear.

"So, you're telling me you know nothing about Terry Fisher's missing cell phone, is that right, Luke? It wasn't stolen by you?"

"No, it wasn't!"

"Well—I believe you, of course. As I'm sure the head will, when you spin her your side of the story. Until then . . . inclusion unit," he snapped suddenly.

"What? Why?"

"Because I say so. You got a problem with that?"

"Yeah! I haven't done anything!"

"And leopards can change their spots," snapped Harmer. "Go!"

Luke argued no more. What was the point? Spinning away, he stalked to the end of the corridor and down the stairs.

The inclusion unit was on the ground floor. Staffed by a duty teacher, it was a special area of the school designed to keep the rowdies away from everybody else. Pupils kicked out of classes went there for a ritual bawling out followed by one of three possibilities: return to class, laughing; a longer spell in the unit; or, supposedly as a last resort, a wait while arrangements were made for the expulsion to be made permanent.

Even before he'd reached the bottom of the stairs, Luke had come up with a fourth option: one of his own design. He didn't know yet, of course, that Terry Fisher's missing cell phone would be found later that afternoon, in the toilet cubicle he'd used for his just-checking-you-got-to-school-safely-darling call first thing that morning, forgetting in his love-struck daze that he'd tucked it behind the toilet bowl while he'd finished his ablutions. No, by the time the cell phone and owner were being reunited, Luke would be long gone.

Instead of turning toward the inclusion unit, he went the opposite way, deep into the ghetto of student lockers. The area had been taken over a couple of years before, having served for a long time as a side entrance. Although no longer used, the door hidden behind the lockers at the far end hadn't been barred and bolted, just locked. It still opened perfectly. All you needed was a key. Or something in your pocket that was as good as . . .

THEY CALLED HIM DIFFERENT NAMES: THE RAT CATCHER, the Roundup Cowboy, the Truant Trapper. What his proper title was, Luke didn't know. Thames Reaches Borough School Attendance Liaison Officer, or something equally incomprehensible. It didn't matter. What mattered was that all the kids he was employed to catch knew roughly where he'd be and when:

> *9:30 or so—around the estates, to catch the late risers.*
> *11:30 to 12:30—Riverside Centre, to catch the shop-lifters.*
> *1 to 2—lunch break.*
> *2 to 3—back to the estates, to snap up the afternoon shirkers.*

After that, he returned to HQ, wherever that was, to fill in his forms and write his reports.

Out in the street, conveniently shielded from the school by a screen of scraggly trees, Luke checked his watch. Nearly midday. He'd head for Riverside. By the time he got there, the Rat Catcher would be off duty and tucking into his ham sandwiches. Luke peeled off his school top and stuffed it into his backpack. Now at least he didn't look as though he should be sitting in a classroom somewhere. Loading the backpack onto his back, he started jogging.

It was like swallowing a dose of fast-acting medicine. Even as he was settling into a steady pace, Luke found his anger at Harmer evaporating. With every step he felt his spirits lifting. The sun peered out from behind a curtain of gray clouds, casting his shadow across the ground. Luke put a spurt on, watching himself accelerate, his arms pumping wildly as if they were draining all the poison out of his system.

Finally he slowed, if only because he was approaching a road he had to cross. That was when the car stopped him. Swinging round from the right, it skidded to a halt in front of him. The passenger leaned out and jerked a thumb toward the rear door.

"What yer running for, Lukey?" Mig Russell grinned. "Only mugs run. Get in, we'll give yer a lift."

Luke hesitated—not for long, but long enough for Russell's smile to vanish. "Get in," he repeated. This time it was a command, not an offer.

Clicking open the rear door, Luke slid into the backseat. The heavy smell of leather told him that this was a new car. In the driver's seat, Lee Young flicked a glance over his shoulder as if he'd just read Luke's mind.

"Nice motor, eh? Just found it at the train station. Window open, would yer believe? Very handy. Owner won't miss it till he gets back on the five-fifteen or whatever train he catches. By then it'll be tucked up nice and safe waiting for its *new* owner to come and collect it."

He gunned the car off again, accelerating fiercely. Beside him, Russell leaned over the back of his seat, sunglasses perched in the middle of his waxed-up hair.

"Convenient running into yer like this, Lukey. Saved us a trip. Yer see, we got a little proposition."

"Want to make use of your special talents, don't we?" said Young.

"Your special lock-picking talents," added Russell.

"Said we'd call again, didn't I?"

"And Lee never breaks a promise."

They said nothing more until Young spun the car round a final bend and stopped suddenly. Luke glanced out of the window. He'd been brought to the rear of what had been a friendly shopping arcade until vandalism and the attractions of the Riverside Centre had driven its customers away. Now all but a handful of the shops were boarded up. Not so the garages-turned-storerooms at the back. They still seemed to be in use—one of them, Luke would have been willing to bet, for giving stolen cars a makeover.

If so, he wasn't going to discover which. He wasn't being taken any nearer. Young had brought him along to make arrangements, not to give him a tour of the business. Switching off the ignition, he swung round to face Luke.

"Don't look so worried, kid. It's a rock-solid job. No danger. Just a gate and a back door."

Luke felt a drip of sweat trickle down inside his shirt. "Wh-why not just break in?"

"Because it's a Sunday job. Leave no signs and we've got twenty-four hours to cover our tracks."

Russell was smirking. "Yer won't have to hang around if you're chicken, Lukey. Just get us in, then yer can cluck off!" He gurgled at his own joke.

Luke's mouth felt dry. He didn't know what to say. Half an hour ago, when he'd stormed away from Harmer, he'd have agreed like a shot. A job with Lee Young and Mig Russell? Dream! Go for it!

But now, with the poison in his mind drained away by the run, he was thinking clearer—just like this last spell in prison seemed to have got his dad thinking clearer; like he'd been doing the same lately. He didn't want to get involved. Trouble was, he couldn't see a safe way of turning them down. He played for time.

"The police said they're watching me. If I was to do it they'd spot you two as well."

Young shook his head. "They won't be watching, kid. Not this one."

"Have too much else on their mind, won't they?" said Russell.

"Controlling the crowds," added Young.

Luke had lost the plot. In spite of himself he asked, "How d'you mean? What's the job?"

Young and Russell exchanged glances. Young shrugged, as if to say, "He's safe. He's not going to tell. He knows it would be the last thing he did."

"A car," said Young finally. "Porsche. Top job. Worth a hundred grand. Man I know's got a buyer all waiting. And he's gonna get what he wants, 'cos the Porsche owner's a total idiot. Keeps a car like that in a simple rented garage. OK, the garage is behind a pair of solid iron gates, but all they've got is a thick padlock holding 'em shut."

"Padlock nearly as thick as the owner," snorted Russell. "So that's your little challenge, Lukey. That and the garage door. We'll do the rest."

"While the cops are all out watching the crowds watching the clowns running in that marathon."

Even before he asked the question, Luke knew the answer. It made him feel sick to his stomach. "Marathon? You mean the London Marathon?"

Young nodded. "Got it in one. London. Big-time. Where else d'yer think this car would be? Reckon there's a few stinking-rich Porsche owners in our part of the world, do yer?"

Russell chipped in, like a caddy picking up his golfer's ball and giving it a polish.

"Man we know tipped us off. Second weekend of every month, Porschie-boy jets off to his place in the south of France leaving his car behind. So we've been doing a bit of staking out, 'aven't we? A bit of planning. The garage is not far from the route those runners take, so the cops will all be looking the other way.

"It's not on the route, though, so we won't be stuffed by them closing the roads we want to use. We can be out and away, no trouble. And with you springing them locks instead of us having to smash 'em, nobody'll be any the wiser till Porschie-boy gets back Monday morning."

"I can't do it."

The words sounded as if they'd been spoken by somebody else, but Luke knew they'd come from him. Why else would Young and Russell be looking at him the way they were?

"I—I'm supposed to be running. In that race. With Jodi—the girl you saw me with that day."

"Then yer'll have to tell the skirt yer can't make it, kid." Young's tone was like ice water. "This job has to be done that day. No other. Yer get me?"

"No, it's—look . . . she's blind. Get it? She's blind."

Russell laughed. "Yeah? Aah, Lukey! And I thought her hanging on to yer was love!"

149

Luke ignored the taunt. "I'm her guide runner, Lee. If I'm not there, she can't run."

"Then she can't run," said Young. "'Cos yer won't be there. You'll be with us."

"But it's part of my service. If I'm not there they'll screw me."

"Tough." Russell shrugged, taking the lead for once.

"Mig, please. Be helpful, eh?" Young was smirking. "This is what yer do then, kid. Tell her a lie. Say you've hurt your big toe or something."

"I can't. She'll know I'm lying. She can tell."

"So don't lie," Young said. "Give it to her straight. Tell her you've already fixed to go out with a couple of your mates—Lee Young and Mig Russell. Yer should think yourself honored, kid. There's plenty who'd give anything to say that."

"I couldn't! If I mentioned your names she'd know I was doing a job!"

The words slipped out before Luke could stop them. In an instant, Young was out of the driver's seat and at the back door, pulling him out. Russell, dumbly following his leader, raced round to grab the front of Luke's shirt and pin him to the side of the car.

Young leaned close. "How would she know that, Luke?" he said. With a speed born of practice, the knife was already between his fingers.

"I d-dunno what you mean," stammered Luke, acting ignorant but knowing he was doomed to fail.

"Mention our names, you said, and she'd know there was a job on. Now how would she know that? How does she know our names?"

"And how does she know we do jobs?" Russell had caught up. "Yer been grassing on us?"

"No! I'd never do that! I told her you were my pals. When you saw me walking her home."

Young was a thug, but he wasn't stupid. "And the rest, kid. There's more, ain't there? Spill it or you'll be needing dark glasses yourself. . . ."

He'd been bringing the blade closer and closer until now it was so near Luke's left eyeball he couldn't focus on it. If he was going to stop Young from using it, he had no choice.

"She was the girl in the parking garage!" gasped Luke, fighting to keep the panic out of his voice. "The one you didn't see straightaway, the one you nearly ran down!"

Mig Russell snorted. "Didn't see!"

No echo could have told Luke more. They *had* seen her. They'd been aiming for her deliberately. . . .

"And yer told her we nicked that car?" snarled Young.

"No! I wouldn't tell on you, Lee! She recognized your voices!"

"I don't believe yer, kid."

Luke felt the chill of the blade touching his eyelid. "She did!" he screamed, panic-stricken. "I told you, she's blind. That's how she remembers people. By their voices!"

The silence couldn't have lasted for more than a few seconds, but to Luke it seemed like an hour as he braced himself for the searing pain of the knifepoint going in. When he felt it lift away, and Young took a step backward, Luke almost crumpled with relief.

Russell still had his great paws on Luke's shirt, though. "Here, Lee . . . Don't that mean the girl could nail us? Y'know, pick us out at an ID parade?"

"Voice parade, yer mean," said a smirking Young. He shook his head. "Nah. The police couldn't make that stick in court even if she could do it."

He was dismissing the thought but, Luke could tell, not with complete confidence. Suddenly, as his doubts loomed larger, he sliced the knife's silver blade through the air. "Maybe we should make sure, though, eh, Mig? Put the frighteners on her as well?"

Luke's panic erupted again. "You couldn't! Not to a blind girl!"

"No?"

Young didn't have to say another word. He hadn't cared whether or not he'd run Jodi down. Now Young's narrow smile was leaving Luke in no doubt that he'd be prepared to cut her without a qualm.

"Lee," he pleaded, "she won't say anything. She won't rat on you. I mean, if she was going to she'd have done it by now, wouldn't she?"

"Says you."

Young wasn't convinced, that was obvious. Luke tried the only thing he could think of, making out that there was much more between him and Jodi than just running. "She wouldn't if I told her not to."

Mig Russell leered. "Got her eating out of your hand, have yer?" He gave an ugly laugh. "Once yer tell her where it is, of course!"

Luke forced himself into a grin. "You could say that."

"Sounds like yer wouldn't want her to come to any harm, kid," Young said. "Am I right?"

"Suppose so, yeah," said Luke.

Young still had the knife balanced between his fingers. Pointing it once more straight at Luke's face, he began moving closer . . . until, suddenly, he snapped the knife shut with a flourish. "All right, kid," he said. "It's a deal."

"Deal?"

"Yeah. Yer come on this London job with us and your blind babe don't get hurt. Right?"

What choice did he have? Protecting Jodi was what mattered. Because he'd meant it when he'd said that he wouldn't want her to come to any harm. He'd really meant it.

Luke nodded slowly. "Right," he breathed.

15

"GO STRAIGHT, JODI."

"Long right."

"Slow, rough ground coming up."

"Speed up!"

"Slow again."

Jodi responded instantly, knowing precisely where they were—coming up to the pedestrian crossing at the bottom of Rigby Road, the one supposed to see you safely over to West Med's so-called recreation area. With its patchy grass and battered play areas, the Rec wasn't much to look at, but it did have one priceless feature—a tarmac path circling its perimeter with a surface like that of most of the roads on the part of the London Marathon route they'd be running.

She heard the gentle squeak of a car's brakes and the peeping of the crossing signal, smiling as Luke didn't go into an explanation of what was going on but simply commanded, "Motor!" meaning "Back up to speed again."

It was part of the code they'd developed over the time they'd been running together. Nearly two months, now. The time had passed so quickly—time in which Luke had developed into such a good guide that even Jodi's father had stopped criticizing him all the time. And that was saying something.

He'd never gone as far as to praise Luke, of course, but he'd definitely changed. Jodi thought it was a bit like the plaster cast on her dad's leg. At the start, that had been tough and inflexible. But, with time healing and the pain subsiding, the rigid covering had slowly been peeled away. Now her father's broken leg was protected by a noticeably softer cast. The slightest setback in the healing process, though, and the hard, unbending version would be back in an instant.

"Sharp right!"

On to the tarmac path now, past the stench of the dogs' poop bin, past the Rec's resident gaggle of pigeons scavenging for scraps around the seats by the entrance, and on. This was about the mile mark. Three circuits of the Rec would amount to another mile. Back home then and they'd have covered the distance.

That was another thing about Luke. He'd gotten stronger. Jodi knew he could outrun her now, no question, just as a good guide runner should be able to. That time at the track when she'd pretended to be whacked-out to save him from total embarrassment was now a fading memory.

"Not much point having a guide who slows you down," her dad had said brusquely whenever she'd complained about him going too fast. But it had been different with her dad. He'd always been trying to prove something, trying to force her into going faster; Luke seemed aware it was more likely to happen if she was having fun, too.

"Long left."

Jodi eased into the gradual bend, which she knew arced

round the Rec's single tennis court. She'd have to suggest a game to Luke, just to hear the shock in his voice! Only then would she let on about the special rattling tennis balls they used to play the game.

Maybe she'd be able to talk her mum into joining them. Mrs. Webb had relaxed as well over the past couple of months. Luke had said as they'd started their run that she'd even waved good-bye!

"Straighten."

On the far side of the Rec now, coming up to the water fountain. Luke had once refused to drink from it, saying the thing looked like it was crawling. "Good thing I can't see it, then!" she'd said, lapping up the refreshing water.

"Stop!"

Jodi obeyed without hesitation. It was another sign of the confidence she now had in Luke. She was surprised, though. Normally she'd have sensed something—an approaching car, people chattering—to alert her that they were approaching a risky situation. This time there'd been no warning at all. "What's up?" she asked.

"I got a problem," said Luke. "Can we sit down?"

Instinct told Jodi that they must be near the solitary bench farthest away from the entrance. Still clutching the guide strap, but taking Luke's elbow as well, she followed him across to the bench. Even over that short distance, she could tell that he wasn't limping. No injury, then. Neither was he whacked-out. His breathing sounded even and regular. She sat down, feeling the bench seat dip fractionally as he joined her.

"Look, this race. What's the arrangements?"

Jodi didn't try to hide her irritation. "Luke, come on! The race is the day after tomorrow! You know what the arrangements are. I've been talking about nothing else all week."

"Tell me again, yeah?"

So she went over it all once more. "The letter from the borough team organizer says we have to meet up at the start. That's in Upper Thames Street, opposite Southwark Bridge. It's only a short walk away from Mansion House subway station. That's on the District Line, so we can get straight there from Town station. Meet us outside . . ."

"Us?"

"Mum and Dad are coming as well, of course," said Jodi. "Aren't yours?"

"No," said Luke quickly. "They can't make it."

Jodi noticed the evasion, wondered about it not for the first time, but didn't press the point. She sensed that Luke's parents weren't the problem here.

"We'll be at Town station by nine o'clock. That should get us to the start by quarter to ten at the latest, giving us plenty of time to change and warm up. The under-sixteens race doesn't start till eleven."

"Eleven?"

"That's the number. In between ten and twelve, right?" Jodi had tried to say it with a laugh, but hadn't quite managed it. Something was up. "So what's the problem?" she asked quietly.

"Eh?"

"We stopped running because you said you had a problem. What is it?"

"Er . . . nothing. Stone in me shoe."

In her mind's eye, Jodi saw Luke lean over, slip off one running shoe, thump it too loudly on the side of the bench, and then put it back on again. "All done," he said when the pretense was over.

Because it *was* a pretense, she knew. Beside her, he was getting to his feet. She took his arm but, instead of standing herself, gripped it tightly to pull him back down onto the seat.

"Close your eyes," she said sharply.

"What?"

"Don't argue. Just close your eyes. Have you done it?" She felt for Luke's face, running her fingers over his eyelids to make sure. "Right. What can you hear?"

"Jodi, I ain't in the mood . . ."

"Answer me!"

Jodi's anger stunned Luke into replying. "I dunno. Birds. Traffic. Kids playing about."

"I hear that lot as well. How about my voice?"

"And that."

"So, what's it telling you? The sound, I mean, not the words."

"You're annoyed."

"At me," he was going to add, thought Jodi. She lowered her hands from his face. "Right. So now you've got an idea what you can tell from someone's voice even when you can't see the person." She turned Luke's way, fixing him with the eyes she could feel but not use. "Which is how I know you're lying."

"What?"

"You didn't have a stone in your shoe. You were going better than me. There was something else you wanted to say. What was it?"

"Nothing. Honest."

"Be straight with me, Luke!"

She sensed Luke bracing himself, as if telling the truth was going to hurt him—or her.

"Something's come up," he said finally. "I—I thought I was going to have to back out. Let you down. But . . . I've just worked it out. I'm OK."

Jodi sensed relief. He was feeling relieved, now. And he was no longer lying to her, she was almost certain of that.

"You will be there?" she said. "You are going to run with me?"

"Yeah. Yeah, no problem. Only . . . look, I'll have to see you there. At the start. Right?"

"Why?"

"Jodi, don't ask. I can't tell you. It's . . . personal. But I'll be there by half past ten, I promise."

She didn't push it any further. What "personal" meant, she didn't know. What she *had* needed to know, the sound of his voice had revealed. He was telling her the truth. It was going to be all right. She smiled. She sprang to her feet.

"Great! So what we waiting for? C'mon, guide runner. We've got another two circuits to do!"

WHEN HE GOT BACK HOME, LUKE DUG OUT HIS MUM'S old A–Z of London maps. It automatically fell open at the page for Wormwood Scrubs prison. Furiously, he flipped to the index, found what he was looking for, then turned back to a different page. Yes, he'd been right. He *could* do it.

Lee Young hadn't trusted him with the details of exactly where this garage was, just said it was Westminster way. Also that they'd be doing it sometime between half past nine and ten, when the crowds were building up and taking the police's mind off other things.

Say ten, then, at the latest. Springing those locks wasn't going to take long. The minute he'd done his bit, he could "cluck off," as Russell had taunted. He'd just about have enough time to jump on a subway train and get back to the starting line for Jodi by half past ten.

It would be tight, but what was the alternative?

There wasn't one.

16

THE SUBWAY TRAIN SPAT ITS WAY INTO EMBANKMENT underground station. On the opposite platform, Luke saw a waiter, complete with tray and glued-on bottle, and a gorilla with his woolly head under his arm. Each had athlete's numbers pinned to their costumes, an unmistakable sign that they were both runners on their way to the southeast corner of London and the full marathon start in Greenwich Park.

Running twenty-six miles must be bad enough, thought Luke—but in a gorilla outfit!

The wonder of it lightened his mood. Only for a moment, though. The tension quickly surged back, tension such as he'd never experienced before a job. Must be the worry of getting to the race afterward, he concluded. He glanced over at the gorilla and waiter once more. It didn't help. Catching sight of their athlete's numbers only prompted the panicky thought that his own number might have come loose. Putting his running gear on beneath his jacket and jeans had been an obvious precaution, in case he was late getting to the start. Unzipping his jacket, Luke revealed the bright orange T-shirt Jodi had given him at their final training session the previous afternoon.

"Jodi, this is gross!" he'd said.

"I'll have to take your word for that, Luke!" she'd replied happily.

Mr. Webb had put his straight-faced oar in then. "All the representative runners will be wearing one."

Luke had turned the T-shirt round. "What's the big B on the back for?" he'd asked, not sure he wanted to hear the answer.

"It stands for 'Borough.' County runners have a C. Maybe you'll have one of those next year, Jodi. . . ."

Mr. Webb had then turned to Luke, handing him a white paper number. "You pin that on the front. Don't lose it. They won't let you run without it."

Now, as the subway train squeaked off again, Luke checked for the umpteenth time that he hadn't lost his number. No, it was still there. Four-one-two-seven.

He looked up to find Lee Young and Mig Russell laughing at him. Sprawled in the seats farther down the car, they were making running motions with their arms.

"And the winner is," mouthed Young, "number four-one-two-seven!"

They were full of it, excited at the thought of what they were going to do, knowing they were just one stop away.

Luke looked away, checked his watch. Ten past nine. Jodi would be on her way by now. At the station he'd had a bolt of panic, wondering if Mr. Webb would have decided to get her there even earlier than planned. Meeting her on the station platform would have screwed things up and no mistake. But all had gone well. They'd caught a train almost immediately and were now ahead of schedule. Luke didn't mind that one little bit. The sooner it was all over and done with the better.

The train sighed to a halt. Westminster. Their stop. The doors hissed open. Out they got. Up the escalator. Through the barriers. Into the watery sunlight for the first impressive sight of the Houses of Parliament. In two hours, Luke would be running past this bit.

A right turn. Along Bridge Street to Parliament Square, a couple of hundred meters maximum, but feeling like much more to Luke. Obviously not to Lee Young, though. Young was cool all right, Luke had to admit that. Hands in pockets, he was showing no nerves at all—not even when Mig Russell hissed, "Jeez, look at all these cops!" Yellow-jacketed police seemed to be everywhere, climbing out of white vans, setting up posts and signs, giving directions.

Young shrugged. "Look like bees, don't they?" he said. "Busy as bees as well. With all this going on, they won't notice us."

Luke hoped he was right. As they walked round Parliament Square and into the shadow of Westminster Abbey, it certainly seemed that way. Back home the mere sight of three prowling teenagers would have been enough to cause a red alert. Here, today, they weren't getting a second glance. It helped that the area was already bustling with sightseers and tourists but, even so, it looked like Young had gotten it right: the police were going to have their minds—and eyes—on other things.

Well past the abbey now. Into Victoria Street, with Lee Young still gazing around as though he was soaking up the sights. But he wasn't. As they reached the next turning on the left, Strutton Ground, he snapped at Luke, "This way, kid."

Down the cobblestoned side street. It was like entering another, quieter world—a world of gray pavements and office buildings closed for the weekend. No more than a dozen paces and they stopped again. Old Pye Street.

A left turn, a slow walk. Here the buildings were different. A mix of blackened stone and red brick, the old and the new, mostly apartment buildings grouped around courtyards. All were protected in some way, either by barriers or fences. Some had garages on the ground floor. Young stopped, pointed at one farther along the street.

"Down there, kid. See it?"

Luke could hardly have missed it. The garage's iron-barred gate was secured with a padlock so big it wouldn't have looked out of place in a medieval dungeon.

"Get going, then," growled Russell. "Signal when you're in."

"What? You're not coming?"

"We'll be here, keepin' a lookout," said Young. "Any sign of trouble and we'll give yer a whistle, right?"

Luke nodded. He'd be able to work quicker on his own, anyway. He checked his watch as he hurried down to the iron gates. Nine thirty-five. They'd taken a slow-paced twenty minutes to get here. He should be able to sprint back to Westminster station in five.

The huge padlock was old but in good condition. Regularly used and oiled. It calmed Luke's nerves slightly. Locks that were rusted and stiff were as much a test of strength as of lock-picking ability.

Even so, it wasn't going to be easy. The thin pick he preferred to work with, and which he'd need for the much smaller lock he could see on the up-and-over door behind the gates, was useless for this. It would be like trying to knock down a wall with a feather.

For this job, Luke had brought a thick nail, filed and hammered into the shape he wanted. Sliding it into the padlock, he closed his eyes and set to work.

See it! Feel it!

Holding the nail between two fingers, Luke used his middle finger to apply pressure, probing nervously as he tried to sense how the lock was constructed.

Gently!

Softly, he bounced the tip of the nail up and down, feeling for the resistance offered by each of the lock's pins. One clicked open. Then another . . .

Had he got it? Yes, he thought so. He gave the nail a final, firm twist, expecting the padlock's solid clasp to spring open.

It didn't move.

Beads of perspiration had broken out on his forehead. One trickled down the side of his nose. He brushed it away.

Relax! He had to relax. He hadn't lost the touch. He was too tense. Had been all morning. It was this race. Nothing more than that . . .

But it *was* more than that. He didn't want to be here,

didn't want to be doing this. The attraction of thieving, the excitement, was gone. In that moment he knew that, somehow, the past couple of months had caused it to dry and shrivel like an autumn leaf. All he wanted now was to get away, to reach that start—and Jodi.

"Come on, kid!"

It was Lee Young, impatiently abandoning his lookout post to come and breathe down Luke's neck. Back at the corner, Mig Russell was giving the adjoining streets a final, quick check before following his leader to the scene of the action—or, rather, inaction.

"OK, OK," said Luke. "Give me a minute."

"You've had ten minutes, kid. Now get a move on."

Ten minutes? Luke couldn't help checking his watch. Nine forty-eight. If he didn't get this done soon, he wasn't going to get to Jodi in time.

"I'm trying!" he cried.

"You'd better be." It was Russell, arriving at Luke's other shoulder.

"Mig's right, kid," muttered Young. "'Cos if you're messing us about, you're going to regret it, and so's that blind-bat girlfriend of yours. . . ."

"I'm not messing you about!"

He tried again, leaning his head against the cool bars of the gate to see if that helped. Slowly he slid the nail back into the padlock, trying to make his fingers, the pick, and the lock virtually join together to become one part of his body. He had to feel, probe, discover its secrets, just as he'd done so often before.

Relax, relax, relax . . .

But never had his fingers felt as thick and clumsy as they did now. He couldn't even keep the nail steady, let alone use it the way he needed. Desperately, Luke applied brute force to a pin that didn't want to budge. More by luck than skill, it was the final touch he needed. With a surprisingly gentle click for a padlock so large, the clasp sprang open.

"About time an' all," growled Russell.

Young was less inclined to waste time with words. He yanked the padlock away, leaving it dangling from one side of the double gate. Pushing the other side of the gate open, he shoved Luke into the small, square yard before following himself. Mig Russell quickly brought up the rear, only half closing the gate behind him.

"Now the next one, kid," said Young, pointing at the door of the garage. He, too, was sweating nervously now. "And make it faster this time."

Luke didn't need to be told. Apart from every second's delay making him later, there was no cover. Young hadn't mentioned that. Any passerby would be able to see him through the bars of the gates. Him, but not them. Young and Russell were looking out for themselves.

"We'll be right here," said Young, sliding into the one corner of the yard that was out of view from the street. Russell joined him.

Luke turned to the lock. It was standard, nothing special, the sort he'd picked dozens of times before. He should be able to do this one in a jiffy and then leave them to it. Putting the thick nail back in his pocket, he took out the slim, supple jigsaw blade that had served him so well and so often. He slid it into the lock.

He tried to picture the lock in his head, closing his eyes again. This action saved him. It reminded him suddenly of the time Jodi had made him close his eyes, taking away his sight and making him focus on what he could hear. Without it, he probably wouldn't have heard the stranger's whistling coming closer along the road outside.

As it grew louder, Luke knew he had to get out of sight. In a panic, he snatched the blade out of the lock, spinning round to race into the sheltered corner where Young and Russell were trying to flatten themselves even more firmly against the wall.

Outside, the whistling was getting even louder. Luke could hear soft footsteps now, too. The passerby must be near enough level with them on the other side of the wall, he figured. Then, suddenly, both whistling and footsteps stopped.

Luke stiffened. Who was it? A he or a she? An answer flicked into mind. Probably a he. Women didn't usually whistle; they sang or hummed.

But what was he doing now? Looking through the gates? Checking the football results in the Sunday paper he'd just bought?

Footsteps again. No whistling, though. And the footsteps were going faster than before. Jogging. Hurrying, for sure. Back the way they'd come, too, as if whoever it was had gotten as far as the gates, then turned round.

"Gone." It was Young, shoving Luke out as he spoke. "Get back to it, kid."

Luke moved slowly, still thinking, still picturing. Who had the passerby been? A neighbor? Somebody who did this regularly—every Sunday morning, maybe? Somebody who'd notice anything different, anything out of the ordinary? Like . . . the sprung padlock Young had left dangling!

"He's gone to get help!" hissed Luke.

He took a step toward the gate, but got no farther before Russell grabbed him, twisting his arm behind his back. Luke cried out in pain.

"Let me go!" pleaded Luke.

"Not till you've done what we want," snarled Russell, shoving him back to the garage door.

"But they'll be coming. The cops. I know they will."

Young grabbed Luke's right hand, which was still holding the jigsaw blade, and yanked it up to the door lock. "Crap. You're trying it on, kid. Now get in there before I break your fingers."

"Why are we bothering with him?" said Russell. "We can force it, can't we?"

"No! It's got to be this way."

Luke's fumbling fingers had gotten the blade back in the lock. But his mind wouldn't work for him. He knew as sure as he'd ever known anything that they were going to be caught. The passerby must have seen that padlock. *And the gates!* Luke could see them in his mind's eye as well, half pushed by Russell so they weren't fully shut.

Not fully shut . . .

In that instant, Luke made his decision. "Let me go, then!" he snapped. "I can't do it with you two leaning on me, can I? Give us some room."

Young released his wrist. Russell let his arm down from behind his back. And, as the pair of them took a step back, Luke acted. Wrenching the blade from the lock, he ran for the gate, diving through the opening Russell had left, then tugging it shut again as they came after him, Young already fumbling for the ever-present knife in his pocket.

Luke ran. Within seconds, he'd reached the cobblestones of Strutton Ground. He spun round to the right, instinctively glancing back to see how far behind they were. They weren't. Young and Russell hadn't followed him. There was only one explanation. They must have decided to force their way into the garage after all and deal with him another day. It was a decision they were going to regret he now saw.

For, just rounding a corner at the far end of Old Pye Street was a man—the whistler, reasoned Luke—with two yellow-jacketed policemen in tow. Had they seen him? He didn't wait to find out.

By the time they'd stopped at the iron gates in front of the garage, Luke was running again.

17

IN THE CAVERNOUS GATHERING AREA—ON ANY OTHER DAY a parking lot beneath an office building—Mr. Webb checked his watch for the umpteenth time.

"He's not coming, Jodi," he growled.

"He is, Dad. He promised me."

Even so, Jodi pinged open the face of her own watch and ran her fingers lightly across the raised hands. Ten-forty. Twenty minutes to start time. She'd already done her warmup. Soon the runners in her age group would be called together by the race marshals before being ushered out to the start line. Could her dad be right? Had he been right all along? Had he seen something that she couldn't, that when it came to the crunch Luke would let her down? She hadn't doubted him before, even when he'd lied to her on that park bench at the Rec. But now . . .

"Sorry! Sorry, I'm late. I . . . I got lost. Went to the wrong place. Had to run." Luke was gasping for breath.

"At least you'll be warmed up, then!" Jodi laughed, more in relief than anything else.

"Save the excuses for later," snapped Mr. Webb. "You haven't got time to go to the changing area now. You'll have to do it here."

That wasn't a problem. Luke removed his jeans, tossing

them into the bulging duffel bag Mr. Webb was holding open. His jacket followed, unzipped and peeled off in a matter of moments.

"At least you haven't forgotten to put your number on," said Jodi's father sourly.

Mr. Webb handed the duffel to another official. Luke knew it was destined for a "baggage bus," to be transported to the finishing area so that the runners could collect their gear at the end of the race.

Everything seemed to be happening in a blur. Jodi was feeling for his arm, attaching the guide strap to his wrist. A megaphone-wielding race marshal was calling for the entrants for the under-sixteens to start gathering behind a striped tape stretched between two other marshals. Mr. Webb was bidding Jodi a hurried farewell, saying he'd see her at the finish. Then he was pushing stiffly through the crowd of parents and spectators on the single crutch he still needed to use. He'd said nothing to Luke.

"Ready?" Jodi smiled. She looked happy beyond measure.

"Raring to go," lied Luke, hoping she was too excited to sense anything—because raring to go he wasn't. His mind was in a whirl.

Even as he'd raced away from the garage, he'd been trying to work out what to do for the best. Had Lee Young and Mig Russell been arrested? They were smart, the top team of East Med. Maybe they'd managed to get away. They'd said they'd cased the place, so the chances were that they'd known of another way out.

But what if they *had* been caught? What then? Would the

police be after him? Were they going to pounce on him and drag him out of the middle of the race? The mere thought of Jodi being left bewildered in the gutter, her dream shattered, made him feel ill.

Don't be stupid! He'd told himself that repeatedly. Running into Westminster station and down the escalator, leaping between the swishing doors of a train that was about to leave, charging off and out and up when the train pulled in after what seemed like hours, then running flat out to the gathering point . . . all the way he'd told himself time and again, *Don't be stupid!*

They wouldn't grass on him. It was the unbreakable law. He hadn't grassed on them. They wouldn't grass on him. No, the only possibility was if he'd been spotted—if one of the police rounding the corner at the other end of Old Pye Street had got a good enough look at him to recognize him again.

Don't be stupid! Luke told himself again. He'd been a ways off when they turned up. Too far away for them to see his face or anything . . .

"Luke!" It was Jodi, tugging at his arm. "They're calling us to the front."

In the one concession to her disability, Jodi had been given a place in the front row of the lineup. Luke guided her up to the colored tape. Two other guided runners were there, both wearing "C"—for County—running shirts. Just the two. He felt a surge of pride.

"Forward!"

The tape-holding marshals were on the move. Out

from the covered gathering area they walked, leading the runners out and left into Upper Thames Street. After a twenty-meter stroll, the marshals stopped, their job done. Now it was the turn of the starter—a huge guy in a tracksuit whom Luke was sure he'd seen running in a big race on television. He wasn't given time to think of his name.

"Three, two, one . . ."

The surge caught Luke by surprise. Even their being at the front hadn't helped. The instant the starter's Klaxon had sounded, excited runners had poured forward as though they were in a sprint race rather than one of over two and a half miles. Before he knew it, they were being overtaken and jostled from all directions.

It made him concentrate, though. After a few stumbled paces, in which Jodi was pushed into his side and almost fell, Luke cast away his own worries and put hers first.

"Steady pace," he shouted. "I'm going in front."

The bunching was so bad that it was the only solution he could think of. Stretching his strap arm out behind him, Luke made Jodi follow him elephant-style. They were still being overtaken, and up front he couldn't see much more than a sea of bobbing heads, but at least they were on the way.

Breathing harder than he would have wished, Luke took it carefully for the first couple of hundred meters.

"We'll be in the underpass, soon!" he heard Jodi call from behind him. "I can feel the road sloping down."

Yet again, she'd picked up on something he'd not even noticed. They'd already started down the incline leading to the underpass that linked Upper Thames Street to the Victoria Embankment, the wide road that would take them along the banks of the River Thames to the Houses of Parliament.

Down they went, moving smoothly, the bobbing heads in front of them sloping away toward the open jaws of the underpass. Luke knew he wouldn't have to tell Jodi when they'd reached it.

"Underpass!" she shouted.

They plunged into the neon-lit tunnel. During the week, this road pounded with the endless roar of traffic passing through it; today, though, it was echoing only with the sounds of feet slapping on pavement and the steady breathing of people running for the sheer joy of it.

"Going up!" shouted Jodi.

They'd done the lowest point of the underpass. And, yes, now they were running up the incline of the two-lane road toward the halo of daylight that marked the exit and was growing larger with every step.

"Moving aside now, Jodi!" called Luke. "Usual position!"

The climb upward, slight though it was, had slowed some of the runners ahead. Others were already regretting their too-fast starts. Gaps were appearing. There was more room to maneuver. Hearing his call, Jodi immediately moved forward slightly so that she was running in her familiar spot at Luke's elbow. He risked a quick turn to look at her face. It was glowing, not with exertion but with delight.

But if Luke thought Jodi looked happy at that moment, it was nothing compared to the squeal of pleasure she gave as they emerged from the underpass and strode into the full glare of the morning sunlight shining down on the Victoria Embankment . . . and heard the first roars of encouragement from the crowds of spectators.

"Listen, Luke!" she cried. "Listen to them!" It was the cry of a girl whose ambition was being fulfilled.

It was like entering a packed stadium. Up to that point, there'd been few spots for spectators. But here on the embankment, with its wide pavements on both sides of the road, there were plenty. People were standing on the bench seats, hanging precariously from the trees, some were even risking a soaking by balancing on the wall separating the road from the river. And they were all, or so it seemed, yelling their heads off.

The cheering hadn't only inspired Jodi, it had given Luke a much-needed boost, too. The events of the morning and the chase to arrive on time had affected him badly. He'd realized that during the short climb up the rise of the underpass. Although he'd kept it well disguised, he hadn't found that section as easy as he should have.

But now, lifted by the support of the spectators lining both sides of the route, he wasn't feeling too bad. He'd have liked to have described the scene to Jodi: restaurant boats berthed along the Thames; the slowly spinning wheel of the London Eye on the far side of the river; the color and spectacle of it all. Best to save his breath, though. He already felt as if it was in short supply.

"Slow left."

They'd just reached the gentle turn the Victoria Embankment makes as it follows the line of the Thames. Within a couple of dozen strides, they were passing Cleopatra's Needle, the huge stone obelisk—one of the oddest gifts ever given by one country to another.

It was there that Luke saw the yellow-jacketed police officer stare at him and say something into his walkie-talkie.

"We'll be coming up to Westminster Bridge, soon!" shouted Jodi, as if she'd memorized every step of the route—which she had.

Luke didn't respond. His mind was elsewhere.

The policeman. Had he really stared at him or was it just his imagination? Had they seen him as he'd run away from the garage? Could one of them have spotted something about him that marked him out as a runner in that day's event—his official orange T-shirt, showing out from below his zipped jacket, maybe? If so, it wouldn't have taken long to get the word round to the cops on race duty. They'd be looking out for him all the way to the finish.

Imagination or not, the thought brought all the tension back. He wasn't even helped by the roar from the crowd as the Victoria Embankment straightened out and they entered the demanding stretch leading up toward the Houses of Parliament. His legs were beginning to feel taut, his stomach tightening. By the time they reached the pointing marshals at the top of the incline, the backs of his legs felt as though they were being stretched on a rack.

"Sharp right!"

The instruction, barked as clearly as he could to tell Jodi they were swinging round into Bridge Street, had made his chest hurt. Gritting his teeth, Luke tried to suck in more air.

"Over halfway!" shouted Jodi.

Luke winced. Another mile to go. Another mile, and already he wanted it to end.

"Parliament Square coming up," shouted Jodi. "What does it look like?"

What could he say? That it looked entirely different from the way it had earlier that morning, that now it was thronged with spectators whereas earlier it had been far quieter; that the police now good-naturedly lining the way had at that time been far too busy to take any notice of three prowling car thieves?

"Packed!" was all he could manage.

It seemed to satisfy her. "I can tell. Listen to them!"

In less than an hour, the throngs lining the route would see the first of the star runners in the main London Marathon. Following them would come the rest of the field: first the serious club runners and then—at a slower, maybe even walking, pace—entrants like the waiter and the gorilla, cheerfully enduring the pain of covering over twenty-six miles so that they could raise money for their favorite good cause. Right now, though, it felt like the spectators had turned up to roar just for them.

"Pick it up, Luke!"

Jodi's call, urging him to go faster, was one he'd been dreading. He glanced at her. She was running more smoothly than he'd ever seen before. Her whole body was relaxed, her stride even and steady. She looked full of running—and he felt empty.

Luke forced himself to speed up. After the punishing

incline of the final stretch of the Victoria Embankment, at least they were on the flat now. His tired legs began to respond. Within meters, they were catching up to a group of runners strung across the road. He had to get past them. Having increased his pace, the last thing Luke wanted to do was slow down again.

"Your way!" shouted Luke.

It was their code telling Jodi to keep running straight but to move to her left, closer to the curb. One of the runners ahead had kicked on, leaving a gap on the inside that was large enough for them to get through. Jodi moved left at once, like a yacht tacking into the wind, until Luke shouted, "Enough!"

They were closer to the crowd than they'd been all race. Not too close to be a danger to Jodi, but close enough to hear individual shouts.

"Keep going, love!" yelled one enthusiastic lady, as though Jodi were her own daughter.

"Not far now," shouted another.

And then, in the middle of it all, a sharp, clipped voice, almost drowned out by the shouts all around it.

"Suspect approaching Great George Street."

Luke swung round, almost losing his balance. Jodi, half a pace behind him, was masking his view of the spectators they'd just passed. Then he saw it, a flash of a yellow jacket—yellow *police* jacket.

They *were* tracking him. He couldn't be imagining it. The two policemen near the garage must have gotten a good enough look at him to circulate his description.

But how? He was so far away and wearing a jacket and jeans, not running gear. How'd they been able to tell he was a runner?

Whatever the answer, one thing was obvious. Rather than haul him out of the race, they were letting him run while they watched every step he took.

So—could he escape? Get away here, now, vanish into the crowd?

Luke looked ahead, beyond the sunless avenue of gray buildings they were running along, to the tree-lined stretch they were approaching. Birdcage Walk: the wide, half-mile promenade that would bring them out virtually at the front gates of Buckingham Palace with only a short distance to go from there to the finish. Birdcage Walk . . .

It ran the length of St. James's Park. If the roads were anything to go by, the park would already be heaving with spectators wanting to see their friends and loved ones race home in glory. That's where he should run for it. He'd be lost in the crowd before the cops knew it. After that, with only a description to go on but no name, they'd be hard-pressed to trace him.

"How's the time going, Luke?"

Jodi's call snapped him back to the present. So wrapped up had he been, so in tune was their running in spite of his aching legs, that for a moment he'd forgotten she was there.

To answer her question, Luke didn't have to look at his watch. Just as she had done for the rest of the route, Jodi had obviously memorized this section. They were running along Birdcage Walk now, and up ahead, its glowing lights clearly visible, was the race clock she must have known they were approaching. Jutting out high above the road, it was ticking the seconds away as they ran, showing how long they'd been going.

"Sixteen minutes, twenty seconds," shouted Luke, continuing as they ran up to it and past it, ". . . twenty-one, twenty-two, twenty-three . . ."

"Then I'm on for a personal best!"

Jodi was panting now, but still moving well. And her smile was still lighting up her face.

Jodi.

Saving himself now would mean leaving her. Could he do that? There was no point in even asking himself the question. He couldn't and he knew it.

So—change of plan. When they got to the finish, her mum would be there, waiting. That had been the arrangement: Mr. Webb to see them off at the start, then catch a subway train to the finish, but in case he didn't arrive in time, Mrs. Webb to go straight there and get a spot as close to the finish line as she could. The moment they crossed the line, Mrs. Webb would be there to look after Jodi. In all the confusion and elation, he'd be able to melt into the St. James's Park crowds and slide away. But only if he could reach the finish line. . . .

He was weak now, desperately weak, but somehow he was managing to maintain the pace. They were approaching one of the traffic islands dotting the length of the road. There was an arrow shape painted on the pavement. His brain was going into automatic. An arrow. What did that mean?

"Ramp!" he shouted. "Take it easy!"

He'd seen it just in time, the surface of the road rising up slightly to make a pedestrian crossing that connected with the traffic island. Jodi slowed a fraction, lifted her legs higher in a light stepping motion as they went across it and down again on the other side.

Luke tried to do the same, but his legs seemed not to want to work. Coming off the ramp, he stumbled, putting his right foot down too heavily onto the surface of the road. Somehow, he managed to stay upright, closing his eyes but not crying out as a dagger of pain shot up his leg.

When he opened his eyes again, his vision was beginning to blur. Ahead, the crowd seemed to be blocking the road. They were right across the road! He couldn't get through them! He was ready to stop, there and then.

It was Jodi who saved him, shouting, "Turn coming up, yeah?"

Turn? Luke tried to focus on the way ahead. The crowd wasn't blocking the road at all. Behind them he could make out gold-tipped railings in front of a huge building with a facade of Portland stone. A stretch of pink pavement was arcing away out of sight and, standing on it, an orange-bibbed race marshal was pointing to his left-hand side. They were at the end of Birdcage Walk, coming up to the turn that would take them along the front of Buckingham Palace.

"Sharp right!" gasped Luke.

From somewhere he'd found the command he needed. But Luke was in a world of his own now, a world racked with pain and exhaustion. Vaguely he could feel his legs moving, his feet pounding on the ground. They'd reached the gold-winged statue of the Albert Memorial. The wide steps at its base were packed with press photographers and TV crews, not cheering spectators, so that for a second it was like running out of a noisy crowd and into a quiet room.

"Here he comes. Orange vest. Number four-one-two-seven, that right?"

Luke heard it clearly. Through sweat-blurred eyes he glanced to the side, saw the policewoman talking into her radio but looking at him. . . .

Number four-one-two-seven? His number. Luke felt as if his mind were detached from his body. His legs staggered on of their own accord as a single picture whirled round inside his head. . . .

The subway train, coming in that morning. Lee Young and Mig Russell making running motions with their arms, Young mouthing "And the winner is, number four-one-two-seven!"

Young and Russell.

The kings of East Med. His heroes. Once.

There was only one way the police could have gotten his race number—from them. Young and Russell had told on *him*!

The dawning of that truth released a burst of fury and energy such as he'd never known before.

"Straighten, Jodi!" he screamed.

They were round the Memorial. The end was in sight, the great square arch with its clicking digital clock and huge lettering: FINISH. The pain didn't matter anymore. Nothing mattered anymore but guiding Jodi across the line, yelling at the top of his voice as they ran flat out.

"Keep going, Jodi! Listen to the crowd! They're cheering you, Jodi! They're cheering YOU!"

And then they were there, across the white line. Staggering to a full stop, Luke released the guide strap and collapsed to his knees. Almost at once, a wildly excited Mrs. Webb was bursting from the crowd, laughing and crying at the same time.

"Well done! Well done, both of you!"

As she hugged Jodi, Luke felt a pair of strong hands take hold of his own arm, helping him to his feet. His legs felt boneless. His head was swimming. Gasping and coughing, he tried to stand. Only then did his eyes, awash with sweat and tears, become aware that the strong hands were attached to arms encased in the bright yellow jacket of a police officer.

Also, from somewhere—far, far away, it seemed—a voice was solemnly saying, "Luke Martin Reid. I'm arresting you . . ."

And then his legs buckled and everything went black.

18

THE GUARD PLUCKED A KEY FROM THE COLLECTION DAN-
gling from the chain at his waist and unlocked the steel door.

He ushered Luke through, waited for his mum to follow,
then did the same himself. The sound of the door being
locked behind them echoed along the corridor.

"In here, please."

Halfway along the corridor, the guard had opened another door, wooden and painted a violent red. Luke and his
mum went in. She'd already pulled the letter from her hand-
bag and was clutching it tightly in her hand.

The room was sparsely furnished with a low table and
four easy chairs. The floor was laid with a thin carpet that
didn't quite reach the walls, allowing the dull, gray tiles
beneath to peep out. A couple of framed pictures hung from
the walls, anonymous shapes in pastel colors. The fluores-
cent light hummed. There wasn't a window. It was a room
that somebody had tried to make welcoming but without
quite managing to disguise what it really was—a waiting
room in a prison.

"Make yourselves comfortable," said the guard hopefully.
"Won't keep you a minute."

When he'd gone, Luke's mum sat down. She started reading the letter again, as if checking to make sure it still said

the same as she remembered, that there was no possibility of things turning out differently.

Luke sat down next to her, stretching his legs out straight. He winced, feeling the sharp pain of the blister on his heel. It must have been growing and getting worse all through the race. Strange how he hadn't felt it. Too much on his mind, he supposed. And by the end—well, by then he was so far gone he could have had a blister on his blister and he wouldn't have noticed. . . .

IMMEDIATELY BEFORE HE'D BLACKED OUT AT THE FINISH line, the world had seemed to Luke to be fading away in a darkening blur; when he'd come round again it appeared to be swaying. Above him, spidery fingers were floating backward and forward in a sea of light blue and white. Beneath him, the ground seemed to be bucking and rolling.

"Take it easy," said a voice near his head. "We'll soon have it sorted out."

He glanced back and up, trying to find the source of the words. He saw the upside-down face of a gray-haired man. He was dressed in a black uniform, a badge with an ornate cross on his front pocket.

Luke's brain began to stir. St. John's Ambulance, he'd realized. They'd had their vehicles on just about every corner. That explained the bobbing about, and the view. He was on a stretcher, looking through tree branches up at the sky.

Other memories were drifting back to him. Jodi being swept into the arms of the ecstatic Mrs. Webb. The solemn-toned policeman. Where were they all? Luke had flicked a glance to the side. They were there. He couldn't see them, just vague outlines, but he could hear their voices. Words and phrases floated across to him, like echoes in a tunnel.

"With two other youths . . . attempted car theft . . ."

Mrs. Webb: "This morning? I don't see how . . ."

"The other two say so . . . reckon he broke in for them . . . gave us his name . . . race number . . ."

He'd been right. Lee Young and Mig Russell. They'd grassed on him. Taken him down with them. Or maybe *instead* of them. They'd made certain he'd be on the way to Markham, all right.

The stretcher began to tilt. They'd reached the ambulance, rear doors open wide. A row of red stretchers alongside, waiting for other customers. He was lifted inside and transferred from the stretcher onto the ambulance's firm bed. At that point, the gray-haired St. John's man had taken charge, volunteer or not.

"Wait outside, please. You, too, officer. You can talk to him when we've got him on his feet again."

"I want to stay with him." Jodi had said it in a way that defied refusal, especially as she was already feeling her way up the double steps as she spoke. "It's my fault he's feeling bad. I made him run too fast."

She was guided to a small seat beside Luke's head, saying nothing while Luke had his blood pressure taken, pulse measured, and was generally checked over. Finally, he had a glucose drink in his hand and the St. John's man had gone outside to tell the police officer, "He'll be fine, bit dehydrated, give him five minutes to get a drink inside him." That was when Jodi had asked for the truth. If she'd added "the whole truth and nothing but the truth," it wouldn't have mattered. Luke had had no intention of telling her anything else.

"They were after a Porsche. They wanted me to get them into a garage."

"Why you?"

"I can pick locks. It's what I'm best at." He tried to force a grin. "That and running." Not lying, though. Not anymore.

Jodi sounded in despair. "So that was the personal matter, was it? Helping them break in. Like you helped them steal our car?"

"I didn't! Jodi, I'm telling you the truth. They forced me to do it."

"Forced you! You're saying you didn't want to?"

"No, I didn't."

"Then why did you? Tell me, Luke. I want to understand!"

"I can't tell you!"

Jodi paused, waiting in the silence. Then she said softly, "It was something to do with me, wasn't it?"

The words might have been a knife, so cleanly had they cut through the remaining strands of his resistance. Luke looked up at the blind girl who could see right through him.

"They said if I didn't help them, they'd get you. Hurt you. They meant it, Jodi. I couldn't let them. . . ."

A thump on the rear doors told Luke his five minutes were up and that the police officer was coming, ready or not. He eased his legs off the bench.

"Take my arm," he said to Jodi. "I'll help you out."

"How are you feeling now?"

Luke smiled a smile that he knew Jodi saw because it was all there, in his voice. "Tell you when the cop's finished with me, eh?"

He led Jodi outside. While they'd been in the ambulance, Mr. Webb had arrived on the scene—to be filled in on the details by Mrs. Webb, no doubt. It was she who came forward at once to usher Jodi away to where her father was standing. As for Luke, his attention was swiftly dragged elsewhere.

"Luke Reid? That is your name?"

The police officer was looking official. He'd also acquired reinforcements. Behind him a policewoman was busy talking into her radio. Luke nodded. He knew well enough what was coming next.

"I am arresting you on suspicion of entering a premises in Old Pye Street, in the company of others, with the intention of stealing a motor vehicle," the officer said, slowly and deliberately. The policewoman moved forward, making a show of getting her notebook ready as he continued: "You do not have to say anything, but it may harm your defense if you do not mention when questioned something that you later rely on in court. Anything you do say may be given in evidence."

In the past, Luke had wished this rigmarole could be made shorter. Now he had cause to be grateful. It had given Mr. Webb time to detach himself from the others and hobble their way.

"Excuse me, officer. What's this all about?"

The policeman turned, frowned, but remained polite in a way that Luke had certainly never experienced from the patrols round East Med. "Can I ask who you are, sir?"

"My name is Allan Webb."

"And are you related to this . . ." The policeman seemed unsure how to address Luke. Mr. Webb saved him the trouble.

"To Luke?" It was the first time Luke had ever heard him use his name. "No. But I'm—well, I'm looking after him today. He was my daughter's guide runner in the race that's just finished."

The policeman seemed sufficiently satisfied by this reply to answer Mr. Webb's original question.

"Then I'm sorry to tell you, sir, that I'm arresting Luke on suspicion of being involved with an attempted car theft at a private garage in Old Pye Street earlier this morning. Two older youths were caught. They say Luke was with them."

Mr. Webb looked puzzled. "Earlier this morning, you say? What time?"

"Just after nine-thirty."

"*Nine*-thirty?"

The officer glanced at the policewoman for confirmation. She nodded in agreement. "According to the witness who reported the incident, yes."

"Then I'm afraid you've got the wrong person, officer," said Mr. Webb.

"Sir?"

"At half past nine, Luke was with me. At the start of the mini-marathon. Isn't that right, Luke?"

His eyes met Luke's, saying as clearly as if he'd spoken the words out loud: "I'm offering you a way out—take it!"

Luke returned his gaze. He was lying! Old man Webb was lying, to save him! Why, Luke didn't know. But he knew what he had to say now. Though his legs were hurting, his mind was thinking more clearly than it ever had before.

"I reckon you need a new watch, Mr. Webb. The one you've got can't be working right. I didn't get to the start till half past ten. At half past nine I was in Old Pye Street, like the officer said."

THE GUARD STILL HADN'T RETURNED. BESIDE HIM, LUKE'S mum seemed nervous, though she had no reason to be. Luke was the one who had the tricky news to give. Hers was good. That's why she'd requested this special visit.

Finally, there was a sound from outside and in he came. Luke's dad. He looked worried.

"What's up?" he said the moment he was in the room. He looked around, saw only Luke, not knowing that Billy and Jade were being safely looked after. "Is it the young 'uns? What's going on?"

"Calm down, nothing's wrong!" Luke's mum was waving the letter she'd been clutching as if it were the crown jewels. "I just wanted you to see this for yourself. We've got a house, Dave!"

The letter had arrived the day after the race. Once she'd stopped dancing, Luke had been able to read it for himself.

Their turn was coming. Billy and Jade, pains that they were, had tipped the balance. Somebody had decided that three children in that little flat were too many—pity they didn't ask me, I could have told them that ages ago, Luke had thought. They'd been allocated one of the houses to be built on the empty field he'd stumbled over on his training runs.

Luke studied his dad. He was looking pleased. More than pleased. He was grinning from ear to ear. He and his mum were holding hands, giggling like little kids.

When they finally calmed down, Luke's dad turned his way. "What d'you reckon, Luke?"

Luke gave him a thin smile. "Good." He straightened, looked his dad in the eye. "It'll be good. So long as you're there. All the time."

"I will be. I promise. I meant it when I said I'm going straight. Eighteen months, that's all I've got left. It's all going to be different then, you'll see." He clutched for Luke's wrist, his eyes moist. "I've got a lot of making up to do. Yeah?"

"Yeah," said Luke. He hesitated, not sure about how to go on. His mum helped him out. "Luke's got another case coming up, though."

"What!" Luke's dad looked furious. "You promised me—"

Mrs. Reid stopped him before he could say any more. "Dave! Hear him out. He got mixed up with Lee Young and Mig Russell."

"Those two!" Luke's dad snorted. "I can remember them with snotty noses and their bums hanging out of their trousers!" He folded his arms and sat back in his chair. "Come on, then. I'm listening."

In the event, telling his story turned out to be more like a dream race than the hard work Luke had expected. He started slowly, uncertainly, but once he'd gotten into his stride, the words flowed out as easily as a top runner floating across the track.

He told his dad everything, from the theft of the 4x4 to the attempt on the Porsche and his arrest after the race. How, somehow, not going along with Mr. Webb's attempt to provide a false alibi had seemed to count even more with Jodi's dad than if Luke had agreed. Mr. Webb had almost taken charge. He'd gone to the police station with Luke and arranged for a taxi to fetch his mum while Mrs. Webb and Jodi had stayed with Billy and Jade. He'd even called Viv and, between the two of them, sorted out the police bail.

"So what's going to happen?" his dad asked. "Markham?"

"Viv hopes not," replied Luke. "And he should know. . . ."

HE THEN DESCRIBED HOW VIV HAD PICKED HIM UP THE evening after race day, the same day the housing letter had arrived. How Viv, before Luke could mention his good news or had even put his seat belt on, had said, "A little birdie tells me that Lee Young and Mig Russell have fallen out, big-time."

Luke had shrugged. "That's good news, is it?"

"According to my little birdie, it is. Seems that when Young grassed you up and told the police you were running in the race, Russell gave him an earful. It didn't stop there. It all got quite heated, the little birdie told me. Heated enough for them to start having a go at each other, mentioning other jobs that had gone wrong. Like a 4x4 that had got burned out instead of making them a tidy sum."

Luke looked at Viv. The probation office was staring out of the windshield, focusing on the road as if a thick fog had fallen to demand his complete attention.

"Mr. Webb's 4x4, it so happens. That'll be on the charge list when their case—their very bulky case—comes up." Viv had whistled a little tune then, as if to give Luke time for the news to sink in. "I don't suppose you'll be surprised they brought your name up where that job was concerned. Not that it matters. You've already been done for that. Served your time, as they say. Well, some of it. . . ."

He'd left it at that until they were seated in the Webbs' tiny lounge. Its appearance hadn't changed much since the time of Luke's first unhappy visit—but the atmosphere had. The whole place felt warmer somehow . . . even before Viv had given him the good news.

"Luke, we're all agreed that the action plan has worked out well."

He was getting nods all round—from Jodi, Mrs. Webb. On the sofa, his leg no longer encased, Mr. Webb was doing likewise.

"So I've written to the magistrates today, recommending that the period for your community involvement be extended to the full four months." He'd grinned as he added, "Which means no spell in Markham."

"Until the Porsche case comes up," Luke had said grimly.

"Hopefully not then, either."

"What! You're sure?"

"No. But with Young and Russell gunning for each other, at least the magistrates will hear the facts about *why* you were there. If they take them into account, together with the good report from this time . . ." He smiled. "You could be OK."

They'd had a kind of party then. Nothing major, just drinks and a few cakes Jodi had cooked up unaided—"apart from me stopping you from putting one blob of dough in the tea strainer instead of a cake pan!" Mrs. Webb had pointed out.

Toward the end, Jodi had taken Viv out to show him how her flowers were getting on. Humming cheerfully, Mrs. Webb had pottered off to do things in the kitchen. Luke had found himself alone with Mr. Webb. There'd been an awkward silence for a while, until Jodi's dad had broken it by raising the very topic that Luke hadn't been able to make sense of since it happened.

"I expect you'd like to know why I . . ." Mr. Webb had paused, searching—Luke assumed—for a word other than *lied*. "Why I . . . tried to come up with an alibi for you."

No point in denying it, thought Luke. "Yeah. I mean, I was grateful. But—yeah, I was wondering."

"Well, for a start," said Mr. Webb, "Jodi told me what you'd told her in the ambulance. That those yobbos had threatened to hurt her. It didn't seem fair that you should get in trouble for trying to protect her."

Luke shrugged unconvincingly. "Life ain't fair, is it? Anyway, you heard Viv. I could be all right when the magistrates get to hear all about it."

"But they're only going to hear about it because of the other two, aren't they? You wouldn't have told them. That would have meant breaking the code on grassing, wouldn't it—and I know how strongly you stick to *that*."

Luke looked up to find that Mr. Webb was on his feet and, if not exactly smiling at him, he wasn't glowering, either. Jodi's father walked slowly to the window, looking out to where Jodi was showing Viv her prowess at negotiating the garden path like a sure-footed gazelle. Luke sensed that Mr. Webb had more to say. He stayed quiet and waited.

"But mostly there was the evidence of my own eyes." Mr. Webb sighed finally, turning back toward Luke.

"How d'you mean?"

"After watching the start of the race, I managed to cadge a lift on the baggage bus. It followed a back route and dropped me at the bottom end of the Mall. Not early enough to get to the finish line but good enough for me to see you both in the distance. I watched you finish through my binoculars. You were out on your feet, weren't you?"

"A bit whacked." Luke smiled.

"But Jodi wasn't. She was having the time of her life, Luke." Mr. Webb took a deep breath, forcing out what he wanted to say. "She was far, far happier than she'd ever been with me as her guide."

He instantly relaxed, as if saying it had lifted a weight from his heart. "You've been good for her, Luke. For all of us. You've taught us that we haven't got a blind girl for a daughter, we've got a daughter who just happens to be blind. Big difference. Anyway, I wanted that to continue. That's why I did what I did and why you'll get our support when this other business comes to court."

"Thanks," said Luke. "I've learned a lot, too."

"Especially about guide running." Mr. Webb smiled. "Which is why I'm asking you to carry on being Jodi's guide."

Luke was stunned. "Even when your leg's better?"

"Even then. But don't worry, I'll still be around doing a bit of coaching!"

"Really?" Luke groaned—and grinned.

"Come on, you can't expect me not to want to be involved with a pair of champions."

"Champions?"

"Yes, champions." Mr. Webb was grinning himself, now. "With your help, Jodi ran that distance nearly a minute faster than she'd ever done it before!"

LUKE SAT BACK, DRANK IN THE WELCOME SIGHT OF HIS PAR-ents not only together but listening to what he'd had to say.

"So, that's it," he said. "Now you know it all."

"You're going to keep on with this running lark then, are you?" asked his dad.

"Yeah. Yeah, I am. Maybe even try to enter some races on my own. Jodi reckons I could do OK. I don't mind either way. Running's great. Gives you a buzz. Better than . . . anything."

Better than stealing things. Better than getting mixed up with the likes of Lee Young and Mig Russell.

The thought prompted him to voice the one real fear he still had left. "Lee Young and Mig Russell. They're not little kids anymore, Dad. They're hard. They're the top two on East Med."

"Not now they won't be," said his dad firmly.

Luke didn't follow. "You don't know them. Things have changed while you've been in—" He cut himself short, only to hear the word come from his dad.

"Inside? Yeah, I know. It's been a waste. But I've learned one thing in here, son. Something people on the outside don't appreciate. We may be cons—thieves, dealers, whatever—but in our funny way, we live by rules. And rule number one is No Grassing." He sat back, knowing that Luke understood, but saying it anyway. "That's why you've got nothing to worry about with Young and Russell. Word travels fast round the Meds. Everybody'll know they've grassed on each other and on you. They won't dare show their faces."

There was a firm rap at the interview-room door. The guard came in, tapping his watch. "Sorry. Time's up."

The three of them got to their feet. Luke's parents embraced. Luke's hair got an awkward ruffle. "All right, then? Problems sorted?"

Luke nodded—until his mum glanced his way. "Oh, yeah." He grinned. "There is one more thing."

"What?"

"The new house. It'll have a garden." Both Luke and his mum were having trouble keeping straight faces. "Luckily, I know a girl who'll help, but when you get out it's still going to mean loads of digging."

"And seed planting," his mum chipped in.

"No problem!" Luke's dad laughed. "Didn't tell you, did I? There's something else I've learned lately. I'm not bad at gardening. Those seeds you brought me, Luke, I sowed 'em in a box like you said. They're coming up a treat!" He was still chuckling as the guard ushered him away.

After he'd gone, Luke closed his eyes, trying to see the rest of his dad's short walk as Jodi would have, in her mind's eye.

He saw him being shown into his cell.

He saw the door closing in on him.

He saw him go to the box he'd placed on the cell's small window ledge, the only spot open to the sun.

And saw, with him, the strong green shoots struggling free from the dark soil and going straight for the light.